SECRET
OF THE
SHADOWS

Also by Cathy MacPhail

SECRET
OF THE
SHADOWS

CATHY
MACPHAIL

BLOOMSBURY

LONDON BERLIN NEW YORK SYDNEY

Bloomsbury Publishing, London, Berlin, New York and Sydney

First published in Great Britain in March 2012 by Bloomsbury Publishing Plc
50 Bedford Square, London, WC1B 3DP

A CIP catalogue record for this book is available from the British Library

ISBN 978 1 4088 1268 6

Typeset by Hewer Text UK Ltd, Edinburgh
Printed in Great Britain by Clays Ltd, St Ives Plc, Bungay, Suffolk

1 3 5 7 9 10 8 6 4 2

www.bloomsbury.com
www.cathymacphail.com

*For all my wonderful
children and grandchildren*

He was walking ahead of me, Ben Kincaid, this boy whose life I had changed. Still young, as he was when I saw him, day after day, sitting at the back of the class. In my dream, he was turning back to me and smiling.

'Thank you, Tyler,' he was saying.

And gathering round him others came, figures emerging from a mist, their hands reaching out to me, softly pleading. 'Help me, Tyler.' They knew my name. They all knew my name. I could hear the tears in their whispers.

And in that moment the dream became something more, something to fear. How could I help them, all these dead people?

I woke up. Glad to be awake.

I dreamed of Ben Kincaid often. Ben Kincaid, the boy who had asked for my help from beyond the grave. I had stepped back into his time and changed the past. Did all the people in my dreams want me to do the same for them? But I wasn't sure I could I do it again? Change the past? It was the question that haunted my dreams . . .

Could I do it again?

1

'It's such a lovely little house, Mum. I wish Gran could have had more time in it.'

We stood outside the shore-side bungalow, me and Mum, looking around at the white painted bay windows, the rock garden and the honeysuckle crawling over the front door. From here, there was a spectacular view down the river as it opened out to the Irish sea. Mille Failte, the wooden sign above the door read. The house had been called that long before Gran had bought it. Mille Failte, Gaelic for a thousand welcomes, and the name suited it. It was a picture postcard house, sitting there on a finger of land on the edge of a wild, rocky coastline. Even wilder today, with the wind lifting the sand, sending it rising like a mist along the shore, and the white-crested waves crashing against the rocks. Gran and her sister, my aunt Belle, had bought it between them so they could spend their old age here together. That dream had been shattered when Gran died of a heart attack.

Aunt Belle was my over the top American aunt, who had sailed off to New York when she was sixteen. She too had dreamed of living here. Home for her was still Scotland. 'The old country', she called it. But now, with Gran gone, Aunt Belle had decided to put the house up for sale and she was coming over for the summer to see to it.

Mum opened the front door. 'Are you sure you don't mind staying here with Aunt Belle?'

Mum and Dad had already booked their trip to Australia when Aunt Belle had suggested flying over from New York. But I hadn't fancied the long flight, and was only too happy to spend the time here with this favourite aunt of mine, helping her sort the house out.

''Course I don't,' I assured Mum. 'She's such a laugh. And I certainly don't want to spend the summer on my own with our Steven.'

Steven, my dippy brother, had just started his apprenticeship as a motor mechanic. All he ever wanted to do was talk about cars.

Mum looked dismayed. 'That's my big worry – leaving

him in the house on his own. He'll have parties every night, I just know it.'

'Our Steven? Are you joking? He'll have a ball. He'll be able to watch his rubbish car chase programmes with no one complaining about them.'

I wasn't sure that was true. As soon as his pals knew he had an 'empty' as we call it (a house with no parents in it), they would descend in their hordes. But I couldn't tell her that. It would only worry her more.

The hallway was dark when we stepped inside. Not even a beam of sunlight managed to struggle through the stained-glass window over the heavy wooden front door. All the rooms were closed up and there was a musty smell in the air.

Mum sniffed. 'Needs a good spring cleaning,' she said. 'It's been empty for too long.'

A family called Forbes had rented it a few months after Gran died, but they had left just a few weeks later.

'Why did the tenants leave, Mum?' I asked. 'Weren't they supposed to be here for a year?'

Mum nodded. 'Yes, it was his job or something. He was called away.'

'Lucky for us they did leave.' I laughed. 'Or me and Aunt Belle wouldn't have anywhere to stay.'

Mum opened the door of the front room. It was dark in there too. The blinds were closed tight and there were white sheets thrown over the chairs and the sofa. Mum pulled one of the sheets back and revealed Gran's favourite blue armchair.

It must have brought back memories for my mum. She sat down and began to cry softly.

'She used to love sitting here, reading her morning paper, watching the river. She said it was the nearest thing to heaven she could imagine.'

I took Mum's hand, trying to comfort her. 'She was happy here, those last few months. That's all you have to remember.'

Mum shook her head. 'I'm not so sure. Something was bothering her before she died. Now I'll never know what it was.'

I'll go back in time and ask her, I almost said, but Mum wouldn't have understood. She didn't know what I had done for Ben Kincaid. No one knew, or ever could know. Not even my friends, Jazz and Aisha or Callum and Adam, or the lovely Mac. None of them would ever know.

I took off my jacket and hung it on the back of a chair. I drew up the blinds and pushed open the windows. The wind tugged at them with such force they flew wide apart. I let out a yell and Mum hurried towards me. It took both of us a lot of effort to haul them shut again.

'You can't avoid the wind here,' she said.

But with the wind came that wonderful smell of the sea and I breathed it deep into my lungs.

'It's going to be so healthy living here. I'm going to go for a jog on that beach every day.'

That made Mum smile. 'If you can drag yourself out of bed before noon.' She wiped her eyes. 'The beds will need changing. But we'll leave the bedrooms till last. Get the rest of the house sorted first, eh?'

'Aunt Belle can sleep in Gran's old room,' I said. 'It's got the en suite. I'll sleep in the other one. It's just as nice as the other anyway.'

How was I to know then, nothing could have been further from the truth.

2

We switched on the radio and sang along with the music as we worked, vacuuming the carpets, dusting and polishing, and in between songs we had a chance to talk too. Mum was so looking forward to catching up with her sister and her husband, out in Australia. Her and Dad had never been there before. The two couples planned to go on a road trip together.

Opposite the living room was a small dining room. It was hardly ever used. I would have had a desk and lots of books in there instead of the oval dining table and high-backed chairs that Gran had picked. It too had a bay window looking up towards the village. We tackled this room next, shifting the chairs and the table so we could vacuum properly. Then we finished the main bathroom off the hall, and the kitchen before we decided to start on the two bedrooms.

'I'll do Gran's room,' Mum said. She picked up the fresh sheets we had brought.

'Are you sure you'll be OK?' I asked her. The room would bring back more memories. So much of Gran was still there.

Mum patted my arm. 'Of course I will.'

The hallway lay in a T shape. At one end was Gran's room and at the other end, next to the kitchen, was the room where I would sleep.

It was dark in here too. Even when I opened the blinds not much light came in. It was a typical Scottish summer's day – windy and wet. The kind of day when lamps are never switched off. I left the door open so some light from the hallway could spill in. I could still hear the music from the radio, and my mum humming happily in Gran's room.

This room would be bright on a sunny day, I thought, with its apple green curtains and duvet cover, and the matching armchair in the corner. There was a tall lamp leaning over the chair and I imagined myself curled up there, reading a book. I was going to like it here, I decided. At least I would when it warmed up. I shivered and started pulling the sheets from the bed.

I hadn't felt cold in the rest of the house, but in here

there was a distinct chill. I called out. 'Mum, this room's freezing!'

I opened the door and went into the hall. 'See – it's warmer here.' I was talking to myself. Mum couldn't hear me over the music, and I shrugged and went back into the bedroom.

I changed the bed, then bundled up the bedclothes. I opened the door and walked down the hall to Gran's room.

'It's freezing in my room,' I told Mum.

Gran's room, on the other hand, was bright and yellow, and warm too. There must be a draught coming from somewhere.'

'Well, we could put the central heating on. Or maybe get you a heater.'

I dumped the sheets into the bag we'd brought for dirty laundry, then took the polish and cloth and walked back to my bedroom.

The door was closed. Hadn't I left it open? And it kept closing. I called back to Mum. 'Something wrong with this door too. It won't stay open.'

She didn't answer me again. Too busy singing along to an old Beatles track.

I had only just stepped into the room when the door swung closed again.

If I wanted to keep it open, I'd have to wedge it with something. I looked around the room and a movement at the window caught my eye. There was a spider crawling up the glass.

If there is one thing I hate, it's spiders. And this was a big one, a big summer spider, its hairy legs stretching across the glass.

And then, I watched as it was joined by another, and then another. They must have been coming from behind the chest beneath the window.

I stepped back. Within moments, there was an army of spiders covering the glass, shutting out what little light there was, plunging the room into darkness. I had never seen so many spiders.

I screamed, 'Mum!' I ran for the door, yanked it open.

She had heard me, was already in the hall.

'What is the matter?'

I pointed to the room. 'It's full of spiders. They're everywhere. We'll have to get someone in to get rid of them.' I pulled her along. 'You go in first. There's hundreds of them.'

She stepped inside and looked around. 'Come here, Tyler.'

I followed her warily inside.

The spiders were gone. The window was bright and clear. There was a break in the clouds and even the pale yellow sun seemed to be making an effort to beam into the room.

'But they were there.' I pointed at the window. 'There must be a nest of them behind that chest.'

Mum looked behind the chest, then she dragged it clear of the window. Nothing. The wall beneath the window was freshly painted white. 'You and that imagination of yours, Tyler.' And she laughed. But I couldn't even smile. All I could think of was, where had all the spiders gone?

She helped me vacuum and dust the room and after a while, we left.

But I should have known then. The door that wouldn't stay open, the cold in that room, the spiders. I should have realised something evil was there in that house. But I didn't. Instead, I went with Aunt Belle to stay there for the summer, and moved into a nightmare.

3

The first day

Aunt Belle arrived the next day. We could make her out a mile off as she came through customs, waving frantically, with her permed blonde hair, her perfect make-up and her long, painted nails. 'Hi there! Hi there!' she was shouting as she pushed through the crowd. As if anyone could miss her. She descended upon us in a mist of perfume, kissing each of us in turn and leaving great scarlet lips on our cheeks. Dad looked embarrassed, but Mum and I couldn't stop laughing.

'It's so nice to be here,' she kept saying, and Mum said she wished she wasn't going to Australia now.

'Nonsense,' Aunt Belle said. 'You'll have a wonderful time. It's been too long since you've seen your sister. Sisters are important,' she said wistfully, remembering her sister, my gran. Then she hugged me again and planted another red kiss on my face. 'And Tyler and I are going to have a great time, isn't that right, honey?'

That night we all went out for dinner. Aunt Belle charmed us all. I hadn't seen her since Gran's funeral, and then, the fun had gone out of her. It was back now. She assured Steven how handsome he was, and that was all the compliment Steven needed to have him eating out of her hand. At last someone was agreeing with him. He thought he was pretty handsome too. And I knew that it pleased Mum and Dad to see how well my aunt and I got on. It would make them feel better about leaving us.

Aunt Belle and I saw Mum and Dad off at the airport the following morning, before we headed down the coast to Mille Failte. Dad had insisted Aunt Belle use his car while she was here, but I was more than a bit wary of Aunt Belle's driving.

'What's this stick here for?' she asked, and when I told her it was the gear stick she scowled. 'You mean it isn't an automatic?' She kept forgetting it wasn't, and the car jerked and bumped all the way. Indicating was something else she just couldn't get the hang of and she kept bawling at other drivers who got in her way. I was sure we were never going to make it to the house alive.

But at last we did. Mille Failte was situated at the far end of a small village on the coast, just twenty-five miles from where we lived. It was right at the mouth of the River Clyde before it opens out to the Irish Sea, distant hills on the other side of the river. On a good day, the island of Arran was just visible in the distance. The village had one main street with a line of fine houses on one side of the road and the shore on the other. We passed the caravan park and then the Riverside Grill on the shore-side before we came to the single-track road that led to the bungalow. I hadn't realised before how isolated it was.

'Didn't it bother you and Gran it was so far away from the main road, on its own out here?'

Aunt Belle brushed that notion aside. 'It's not so far away. A good fifteen-minute walk is all and you're back on the main road. And bothered? In this little village? A crime wave here is when two five-year-olds have a fight in the school playground.' She had a laugh that bubbled and it made me laugh too. 'No, honey, for us the remote-ness only added to its appeal.' She grew silent as we drew near the house, and I knew she was remembering Gran, just as Mum had.

She cried when she stepped into the house. Her tears upset me too. It wasn't like Aunt Belle to cry. She was usually so much fun. Gran used to say Aunt Belle had never grown up. I just think she never wants to grow old. She loves being with young people, maybe that's why she and I get on so well.

I let her cry. I made her a cup of tea and took it into the front room and found her sitting in Gran's blue armchair.

Finally, she sniffed and said, 'Your gran wouldn't have wanted me to cry too much. It's just we had so many plans, your gran and I.'

'You could still come here and live. Not bother selling the house. Wouldn't you like to do that?'

She shook her head. 'Not without your gran. It wouldn't be the same. Maybe it wasn't meant to be. Some things aren't, you know. It's made me realise I really am an American now. A New Yorker.' She reached out and touched my hand. 'But you and I are going to have a lovely time here this summer, I'm looking forward to it.'

I thought she might cry again when I carried her case into Gran's bedroom, but her crying was done. 'We both wanted this room, you know. We decided to toss for it. Can you imagine? I think your gran cheated. Used a two-headed coin! She said she should have the en suite anyway, because she was older than me.' She still laughed at the memory.

Aunt Belle felt the cold in my room too, as soon as we entered it. 'It wasn't cold like this when I slept here. I was only here for a couple of nights, of course. But I think you're right, Tyler, there's a draught coming from somewhere. We'll call someone tomorrow, get it sorted.'

I was going to tell her about the spiders, but it sounded silly now. I still couldn't explain where they had gone. All my imagination. While she gushed over the view from the window, I dragged the chest to the bottom of my bed. I would feel a lot better if the space under that window was clear.

Mum had filled the fridge and the freezer with food for us, but Aunt Belle decided that on our first night we should have dinner at the Riverside Grill.

It was late when we came back in, but still light. I got into my cosy jammies, and Aunt Belle appeared in the living room wearing a glamorous, purple silk dressing gown and high-heeled slippers. She was also carrying a dummy head with a blonde wig on it.

I burst out laughing. 'I didn't know you wore a wig!'

'Oh goodness yes.' I saw then her own hair was thin, wisps of blonde hair tinged with grey. She looked around the room. 'Where can I put this so it gets some air?'

No wonder she made me laugh. She placed her wig gently on the windowsill.

'Aunt Belle, even without your wig you look like a film star,' I said.

'I always like to feel good, honey. Your gran used to laugh too.'

It was even later before we said goodnight. I went into her room with her and sat on the bed, and we drank hot chocolate and talked. By the time I was closing her door her light was out, her eyes already shut.

I walked down the hall to my room. I had decided to wedge the door with a heavy book, but the room itself was in shadowy darkness and I wished I had left the bedside lamp turned on. It seemed the whole house was dark and silent. I felt alone.

The cold hit me as soon as I stepped inside, as if someone had blown their icy breath towards me. I jumped into bed and pulled the duvet tight around me. I switched on the bedside lamp and its light sent out a warm glow. I could see myself in the tall mirror in one corner, a girl with long fair hair and freckles, and blue eyes. I smiled and my reflection smiled back.

It was a lovely little bedroom. Yet it was so cold. My

nose was like an ice cube. I pulled the duvet almost over my head.

I was tired, I decided, and needed sleep. I switched off the light and slid deeper under the covers.

I don't know what woke me, perhaps the wind outside or the sound of the sea rushing into the shore. But I opened my eyes and felt sure I was not alone. Someone was in the room with me.

'Aunt Belle?' My first thought was that she had woken up and come in, but there was no answer. I sat up and rubbed my eyes.

The door was closed.

I had wedged it open. How had it managed to close?

And then, it seemed there was a movement in the corner, in that armchair. My eyes flickered towards it. It looked almost as if someone was sitting there. A dark figure. I blinked, trying to focus. It did look as if something was there. And not just sitting, but moving. A shadow stirring into life. My hand was shaking as I reached out to switch on the lamp. Someone was in that corner, I could swear they were. Ready to stand and take a step towards me.

I flicked the switch and light filled the room. The

chair was empty and behind it was only the tall lamp with its lopsided shade. It leaned over the back of the chair like a drunken man. I felt stupid. I had obviously mistaken the lamp for a figure. I stared at it for a long time, waiting for it to move, for the shade to topple and fall. But nothing happened. And for a second there, in the midnight of my room, I remembered Ben Kincaid and the statues that used to turn to watch me.

I waited for another sign, but nothing came, nothing changed. Of course nothing changed! Strange things didn't happen in bright little bungalows like this. They happened in great Victorian mansions. Or in old schools, with long, dark corridors. Not here. I was being silly, I decided.

But I still slept the rest of the night with the light on.

4

The second day

All my friends came to the house the next day. It would be the last time I would see them before they went off on their respective holidays. I'd told them so much about Aunt Belle they were all dying to meet her.

Aisha and Jazz arrived first. 'Hope you don't mind us turning up like this,' Aisha said. Jazz didn't bother apologising. She was sure we would be happy to see her. Out of school, she went mad with her style. Her black hair stuck up in spikes and her eyes were smudged black too. She was so different to Aisha, with her long brown hair held back in a neat clasp. Although maybe Jazz was just what Aisha needed to put the fun into her life.

'The boys are coming later,' Jazz said, chewing gum, pink through her bright white teeth. 'We thought we could phone for pizza or something.' She turned to Aunt Belle. 'You don't mind, do you?'

21

Aunt Belle laughed. 'Mind? Of course not. And forget about pizza. I'm going to make a spaghetti Bolognese for us all.'

'The boys are coming?' I mumbled.

Jazz gave me a playful push. 'Including Mac. Don't worry.'

'Mac?' Aunt Belle said, lifting a painted eyebrow.

Jazz smiled. 'She hasn't told you about Mac? He's her boyfriend.'

'Not exactly my boyfriend, he's just . . .'

Jazz shook her head. 'He's her boyfriend, Aunt Belle.' She was already adopting my aunt as her own. She turned to Aisha. 'Isn't that right?'

''Fraid so. We just don't know what she sees in him.'

Aunt Belle was delighted. 'Oh, I am looking forward to meeting him,' she said.

'It's a bit quiet here, isn't it?' Jazz said, peering out of the window at the sea. 'Wouldn't like to be here by myself on a dark and stormy night.' She gave me another push. 'Bet you could write a great story about this place, Tyler. You know, one of your creepy ones, about ghosts and ghouls.'

'It used to be even more remote.' Aunt Belle joined her at the window. 'When it was first built, it was completely isolated.'

Jazz grinned. 'I think I prefer it this way. Aunt Belle,' she went on, 'I have seen too many films where the beautiful heroine is alone in a remote house and a mad axe man is after her. And I always see myself as the beautiful heroine.'

She'd have to fight Aunt Belle for that role, I thought.

I had planned to tell them all about the spiders and the weird feeling that had woken me up in the night, but finally decided against it. It seemed absurd now, and Jazz would only say it was another of my stories. I couldn't hide the cold though. As soon as Jazz and Aisha walked into the room, they felt it.

'Where is that draught coming from?' Jazz asked, rubbing at her arms.

I swung round to answer her and gasped. There was a shadow on the chair. It sprang to life, leaping from the seat. I stumbled back.

But it was only Aisha. She caught my arm. 'Hey, Tyler, what's wrong?'

'I–I didn't see you sitting there. You gave me a fright.'

Aunt Belle came in just then, carrying an electric heater. 'This is going to stay on till this room warms up.'

Aisha settled back in the chair again. 'I love this room. I would sit in here at night and read my book.'

'And think about Callum . . .' Jazz nodded to Aunt Belle. 'That's her boyfriend.'

'And have you got one, Jazz?' Aunt Belle asked.

'Who'd have her?' Aisha said.

'She scares boys too much,' I said, and we laughed and all of a sudden the room didn't seem frightening. No one else seemed to feel the strangeness in here. Only me. I decided then that in the dead of night when I woke up and it was cold and I imagined something in that chair, I would remember this moment, remember Aisha sitting there laughing, and I wouldn't be afraid again.

5

'Who does your nails?' Jazz asked Aunt Belle, when we went back into the front room. She lifted Aunt Belle's hand and studied them with admiration. 'They're lovely.'

'I do them myself, dear. Always have. I think I should have been a beautician. Missed my vocation there.'

'What did you do?' Aisha asked.

'I was a waitress at a Republican club in New York,' she told them proudly. 'I met presidents and film stars and so many interesting people. I've had such a terrific life, and two wonderful husbands.'

I giggled. 'My aunt Belle always manages to get double her share of everything!'

Aunt Belle laughed too. 'I was born lucky,' she said.

'Tell us about when you first went to America,' Aisha said eagerly.

They didn't need to ask Aunt Belle twice. She loved sharing stories about her past.

'Maybe you could do my nails at the same time.' This was Jazz, holding out her black painted nails to my aunt.

And that was the way we spent the afternoon, Aunt Belle sitting happily with her nail polish collection, filing, polishing and painting me and my friends' fingernails, and telling them wild tales of her early days in New York. I was sure she made half of them up, but who cared?

I knew she would be a hit with them.

'When are you going off on holiday?' I asked. Jazz was off to Spain with her family, Aisha to Egypt.

'In a couple of days,' Jazz said, admiring her nails.

'We're all going to be away. The boys are going on holiday too. You'll be all alone, Tyler,' Aisha said cheerily.

Alone. For a second the word made me shiver, but I shook the feeling away.

'Not with Aunt Belle here,' I said.

The boys came just in time for dinner. If Aunt Belle had been expecting Mac to be a kilted Scotsman and not a skinny Asian boy, she said nothing, just smiled and winked at me in approval behind his back.

Aunt Belle's spaghetti Bolognese was so good. We

ate in the dining room round that oval table – Aunt Belle insisted we have dinner there – and we talked and laughed, and every so often, Mac would look over at me and smile. Jazz spotted him one time and groaned. 'There's something wrong here,' she said. 'Aisha and Callum, and Tyler and Mac. But what about poor little me?' She grinned at Adam and made an effort at fluttering her eyelashes. 'You could be my boyfriend, Adam. You've always fancied me, haven't you?' She puckered her lips, offering them to Adam.

He shrank back from her. 'Me? I'd rather kiss a cobra.'

Jazz hissed like a snake. 'That could be arranged.'

They were always winding each other up like that, but I was sure deep down they did like each other. It was only a matter of time till they both realised it.

Aunt Belle insisted they go before it was too late. 'It's a lonely road,' she told them.

'I thought you told me it was only delinquent five-year-olds we had to worry about here?' I giggled.

Jazz put on a spooky voice. 'But at night, who knows what horrors could be lurking in the shadows.' She laughed. We all did. But in that moment, despite the light and warmth of the dining room, the words 'lurking in the shadows' made my skin break out in goose pimples.

It was a warm summer evening, with the orange sun setting over the river. I brushed away any fear I had. What bad things could happen in this lovely house? With my cheery aunt Belle here beside me?

My friends left soon after dinner. I felt a knot of fear in my stomach I couldn't explain as I watched them walk up that long road to the bus stop. Mac looked back once and waved. And then they were all gone, swallowed up in the distance. Almost as if they had vanished from my life. Why was I feeling like that? They were only going on holiday. Why did I suddenly feel so isolated?

Aunt Belle must have noticed my mood. She slipped an arm around my shoulders. 'Come on, let's go for an ice cream. That'll cheer you up.'

We brought a big tub of ice cream back from the cafe in the village, and we sat on the patio outside the kitchen, savouring it and watching the sun sink behind the hills.

'The evening your gran and I came here to view this house, it wast just like this. We couldn't believe our luck. We'd found the perfect house. Couldn't believe it hadn't been snapped up by someone else. That it had been

28

empty for so long. That it was so cheap! So we signed for it the very next day.'

She got to her feet. 'Right, time for bed, for me at least.' She yawned. 'I feel so tired. Must be jet lag.'

I sat up for a while after she went to bed. There was a film on television. A strange story about a missing boy. Had he run away? Had he been kidnapped? Who was guilty? As it neared the end and it was clear the boy had been long dead, that he was a ghost back for revenge, I wished I hadn't stayed up to watch it. And I knew then I had only been putting off going to bed. I kept imagining the closed door of my bedroom, and couldn't stop thinking about what was behind it.

Nothing, Tyler! I kept telling myself. There was nothing inside that room.

I got myself a glass of milk from the kitchen and stood for a moment outside my room before I opened the door. I had left the light on deliberately, so I could see every corner. It was still cold, even with the heater blasting away. And when I stepped inside, after only a few moments the door still swung shut. As if a dead breath had blown it closed.

There was something wrong here, in this room. I only wished I knew what it was.

6

I wedged the door open again, climbed into bed and tried to concentrate on the next chapter of my book. But I was tired and so I turned off the bedside lamp after only a few pages. The slashes of moonlight coming in through the window reassured me, and the memory of Aisha sitting laughing in the chair in the corner too. I could make it out in the silver light, and the lopsided lampshade made it look faintly comical. I could even hear Aunt Belle's gentle snoring from her room. There was nothing to be afraid of here, I told myself. And with those comforting thoughts I fell asleep.

The duvet was right over my head when I woke up. What had woken me? Was it a sound? I listened, but all I could hear was the comforting rush of the incoming tide, and the early cawing of the seagulls.

Yet, there was something there. Something in the atmosphere of the room. And it was even colder than I remembered. I dared a peek over the duvet.

Darkness.

And that's when I realised the door had closed again. I had wedged it open, and now it was closed. How could that happen? Was that what had woken me? The sound of that door clicking shut.

There was a cold sweat on my brow. My eyes were drawn to that chair in the corner. I tried to make out what was there in the darkness and it seemed to me that the chair was enveloped in that same strange shadow. I stared at it for an age.

And the shadow moved.

Something stirred in that chair. Something was watching me. I saw no eyes. There was nothing but shadow, yet I was convinced it was watching me. My teeth began to chatter and my hand trembled as I reached for the lamp. In my mind's eye, I saw another hand, its skeletal fingers reaching out to stop me.

With one flick the lamp was on. Light flooded the room and I leapt from the bed.

I stood in the corner, back against the wall. The chair was empty. Of course the chair was empty. It was only a harmless, inoffensive chair, and a door that wouldn't stay open. In the light, I refused to think otherwise. Still, I never took my eyes off the chair as I moved towards the door, telling myself all the time I was foolish.

The handle of the door was ice cold. I turned it slowly, pulled the door open, and backed out of the room and into the hall.

I stood, rubbing my arms, staring into the gloom of that room, half expecting something or someone to materialise there.

And then, another shadow made me jump – a shadow in the kitchen.

At that moment the door was pulled open wide. 'I thought I heard you.' It was Aunt Belle, in her purple dressing gown. 'Couldn't you sleep either?' She held up the kettle. 'I'm just making myself a cup of tea. Do you want one?'

I looked back into my room at that green chair and I shrugged. It was as if a veil had been lifted. Normality had returned. How stupid I was being. Bad dreams and my wild imagination. That was all.

7

Aunt Belle and I sat in the kitchen with our tea – in a china teapot with china cups and saucers. Aunt Belle had no time for mugs, she said. And we talked until the red lights of dawn brushed the sky.

'I think it's the cold in that room that wakes me up,' I said, almost talking to myself. I didn't want to alarm Aunt Belle with stories of moving shadows on chairs. 'And the door keeps closing all the time.'

'Subsidence,' she said at once. 'This is an old house, built in the 1920s. What with its age and being right next to the sea, there's bound to be subsidence . . . I think I remember your gran mentioning that to me once.' She looked thoughtful, trying to remember. Finally she gave up with a shrug. 'We'll get a carpenter in about the door. See what he can do.'

Subsidence made the door close, and it was just a gap

in the woodwork creating the draught. Down to earth, sensible explanations. They reassured me. I was happy to believe them.

'Jet lag. I feel so tired,' Aunt Belle said, and she yawned. 'I can only sleep a couple of hours and then I'm awake again.'

I wondered then if there was something of the shadow in Aunt Belle's room, but she dispelled that notion straight away. 'I love that room. I feel as if your gran's in there with me. We always had so much fun together.'

I remembered then that my mum had told me once that Gran had a gift, a gift for seeing the dead, and that she'd passed that gift on to me.

'Did you ever think Gran might be psychic, Aunt Belle?' If anyone would know more, surely it would be her?

She spluttered into her tea. 'Your gran? You've got to be joking. She was always taking the mickey out of me because I was the one who believed in all that stuff. I used to go to seances and I was told once I was the rein-carnation of an Egyptian princess, and do you know what your gran said? "Oh, of course, Belle, you would never have been the reincarnation of a kitchen maid, would you? You'd have to be a princess." She thought I was too gullible and all that kind of stuff was just nonsense.'

I laughed. Aunt Belle, a kitchen maid? Never.

'Mum said she felt Gran wanted to tell her something before she died,' I went on. 'Something was bothering her. And Mum always regrets she didn't get the chance to ask Gran what it was.'

Aunt Belle looked thoughtful. 'It's funny you saying that, because the last letter I got from your gran she said something similar.' She got to her feet. 'I've got the letter in my case. I'll show you.'

As I waited I imagined my gran, alone in the night, here in this house, with its ice-cold room, and a door that closed of its own accord. Were those the things that had been bothering her?

Aunt Belle came back, pulling the letter from a blue envelope. I felt a lump in my throat when I saw my gran's neat handwriting.

Aunt Belle pointed a finger at one of the pages. 'It's all about how much she loves it here, until you get to this bit.'

She handed me the letter and I read it aloud.

"*You'll love it too, Belle. We can walk on the beach every day, and watch the sun set every night. There are a few things about the house that are concerning me. I won't bother you about them yet. I can't sleep at night. I think this house has a history. I'm going to find out what it is.*"

'Of course, being me, my first thought was it was something supernatural that was concerning her,' Aunt Belle went on. 'I was reading a horror story at the time, all about a house that had evil in its very stones. Then I remembered it was your gran writing this letter. She probably meant the plumbing was acting up, that's what was keeping her awake. Bad plumbing. Your gran always said I had an overactive imagination.'

'That's what people say about me too, Aunt Belle. I think I'm just like you.'

'I'd be very proud if you were,' she said, smiling.

'But what if you were right . . . and there *was* something in the house. You can't sleep and neither can I.' I just stopped myself from mentioning the shadow I thought I had seen in the chair.

Aunt Belle patted my hand. 'I've got jet lag, and your room's a refrigerator. That's why we can't sleep. There's nothing bad in this house. Your gran's here. I can feel her everywhere. She's watching over us.' She took the letter from me and folded it back into the envelope. 'Now, why don't you come into my room till it's time to get up.' She giggled. 'It'll be like a girls' sleepover.'

It was. We lay together as the sun rose higher in the

sky and I listened and laughed at more of her stories about her life in America. And I thought, Aunt Belle's right. Gran is here, in this room, listening and laughing along with us.

8

The third day

By the time we surfaced it was nearer the afternoon and after a very late breakfast we went for a walk along the beach.

'Gran used to do this,' I said. 'She said she'd never felt so healthy.'

Yet, she had died here, another voice in my head whispered.

Aunt Belle had promised we would go out for an Italian meal that night, but by the evening her tiredness had come over her again. So instead we phoned for a pizza delivery and after we'd eaten it, she suggested an early night. 'We probably both need it,' she said. 'We hardly slept a wink last night.'

I sat in the front room watching television long after she went to bed, anything to put off the moment when I would have to go into that room.

I would not be afraid, I kept telling myself. I refused to let a draught in an old house, and subsidence, and a shadowy corner make me afraid.

But, just in case, I would sleep with the light on.

Tonight, I closed the door. What was the point of wedging it open when it would only close again anyway? I tried to read in bed for a while, but my eyes kept closing and I fell asleep. Even when the book slipped out of my hand and hit the floor, it didn't wake me.

But something did.

I opened my eyes to darkness. The room was icy cold. I blew out a breath and I could see it form a misty cloud in the air. My eyes searched out that corner, that chair, the shadow. I couldn't stop them. How could it look so like someone was sitting there? A shape in the darkness, watching me, even though I knew no one was there. Why was my imagination playing these tricks on me?

I blamed Ben Kincaid. Making me believe I had the power to see the dead, to summon them, to change the past.

But who had died here? My gran had died in hospital, not here. And anyway, she would never frighten me.

This house has a history, the words in Gran's letter repeated themselves in my head. Maybe Aunt Belle had been right with her first thoughts. What Gran had been referring to had nothing to do with the plumbing and more about someone who had lived here, who had died here.

All the time these disturbing thoughts fluttered through my head, I stared at that chair till my eyes stung. Till I was sure I saw a movement and I jumped. Something *was* moving there. Rising from the chair. Coming towards me.

And it was then I remembered that I had left the light on and now it was dark, and that realisation made me throw back the duvet and leap from the bed. I pulled the door open and I could almost swear I heard the whispered words:

'I missed you last night.'

9

The fourth day

I slept the rest of the night on the sofa in the living room. Nothing disturbed me there. It was late when I got up. After eleven o'clock. I wondered at the silence in the house. Aunt Belle was still asleep, but she had been up at some point. There was a glass of water beside her bed, and a broken strip of paracetamol tablets. I felt her brow. It was cold to the touch, and she looked pale.

I made some coffee and took my mug into my room. In daylight, I wasn't afraid here. I could have a shower and get dressed, perhaps walk to the shop for some fresh rolls before Aunt Belle even woke up.

I had put some of my clothes into the chest at the bottom of my bed. I bent down and opened the lid, resting it against the bed and reached in for a T-shirt. In that instant, the lid flipped down. I pulled my hands away but I wasn't quick enough. There was a catch on the old chest made of sharp, raw metal, and as I drew my hands back it left a long gash on my arm. Bubbles of blood formed in a ragged ridge. I fell back as the pain hit me. I got to my feet, clutching my arm, and hurried into the kitchen.

It had all happened so fast it had taken my breath away. The way the lid had snapped down so unexpectedly, almost as if someone had thrown it back deliberately. I shook my head free of that notion. It was nonsense. It was just a stupid accident, nothing more.

I had a wad of kitchen roll pressed to my arm when the doorbell rang. I pulled on a dressing gown and then opened the door to the tallest policeman I had ever seen. His jaw jutted out so much you could have used it as a foothold.

He took one look at the blood seeping through the paper towel, and said, 'What happened here?' His voice was as deep as he was tall.

'I just cut my arm,' I said, holding it against me. 'Stupid accident.'

I was going to explain about the sharp catch on the chest when a terrible thought came to me and I forgot everything else.

A policeman at the door. Had something happened to

my mum or my dad, or to Steven? I drew in my breath. 'Is something wrong?'

He shook his head. 'Nothing at all. I'm only here because this house has been unoccupied for so long, and with it being a wee bit remote, we like to check up on it.' He nodded to my arm. 'You're sure that's OK?'

'Yes. The bleeding's probably stopped already.'

Just then Aunt Belle came hurrying down the hall. The doorbell had obviously woken her up. Her silk dressing gown flew behind her, and she'd remembered to put her wig on. She took one look at the policeman and had the same thought as me. 'Oh my Gawd! Who's dead?'

I saw the beginnings of a smile on the policeman's face. 'Not a soul, madam. Sorry to alarm you. My name's Sergeant Ross. Just checking up on the house. Making sure everything's OK here. See the young girl's had an accident.'

Aunt Belle turned to me. 'What did you do, honey?'

I was embarrassed by the fuss. I tucked my arm behind me out of sight. 'It's nothing. It was just a silly accident. I caught it on that old chest. I wasn't paying attention.'

Aunt Belle smiled. 'She's always in a dream is our Tyler,' she said to Sergeant Ross. 'She's going to be a writer,' she added proudly.

I was so mortified when she said that, I felt myself blush.

'You've got a good imagination then,' he said kindly.

Aunt Belle answered for me. 'And what an imagination! She can make up a story just like that!' She snapped her fingers. 'Out of anything.'

Now that she saw my wounds weren't life threatening, she turned her charms on the sergeant.

'How kind of you to look in on two lonely females.'

'Well, this part of the job is a pleasure.' He was equally charming. 'You're an American then?'

'Yeah, from New York. But I was born here.' She clutched the dressing gown around her. 'Sorry to appear like this. Had a bit of a lie-in. I think I'm suffering from jet lag.'

He looked around the hall. 'You plan to live here?'

She shook her head. I hoped her wig was on tight and wouldn't fly off into the sergeant's face. 'No, I'm here to sell it.'

'Well, it's a lovely wee house. You should get a good price for it. Been lying empty for too long.'

He left then, telling us to get in touch if we ever needed him.

'Aunt Belle, you were flirting with him!'

She linked her arm in mine. 'It will be a sad day, honey, when I'm too old to flirt with a good-looking man.' Then she laughed. 'Come on, let's get a plaster on that arm of yours.'

10

After lunch Aunt Belle still didn't feel one hundred per cent. I told her I would walk to the shop in the village for some fresh milk while she had a nap. 'Get me a pick-me-up, would you?' she said. 'Something to give me a bit of energy.'

The village shop was, rather grandly, called The Delicatessen. It was a tiny little shop on a corner and it sold just about everything from stamps to medicine.

The woman behind the counter had a tangle of black hair and a distinct Italian look. *Mrs De Luca*, her badge proclaimed.

There was an aisle for pharmaceutical products and I asked Mrs De Luca if she could recommend a pick-me-up. Something natural, to give my aunt a bit of energy. She suggested some kind of vitamin tonic, and after reading the label and checking what was actually in it, I bought it. Mrs De Luca had a cheeky wee face and as I handed over my money she stared at me. I was a stranger in the village and she was suspicious of strangers.

'You staying at Mille Failte?' she asked, and I could tell by her tone she already knew I was. She looked like the kind of woman who knew everything, and what she didn't know she would find out.

'Yes, I'm there with my aunt,' I told her.

'Is that aunt of yours selling it?'

Nosy old busybody, I thought. I nodded.

'Is it going up for sale soon?'

It seemed she didn't need an answer. She answered herself. 'I suppose it will be. I've told my niece. She'd love to buy it. Do you know what kind of money that auntie of yours wants for it?'

I hesitated again. She would probably tell me herself in a second. But she didn't. She waited for my answer. I thought she had a bit of a cheek even asking, but I couldn't have answered her anyway. I only shrugged. 'Haven't a clue,' I said.

Then it occurred to me that this woman was nosy enough to know all about our little bungalow and who had lived in it before us. Gran had said this house had a history, and I wanted to know what it was. 'Can you tell me who used to live there before?'

'Oh aye,' she said. 'It was a merchant seaman that had it. He had it for years, let it go to rack and ruin. He was never there, always at sea. Pity 'cause it's a lovely wee house. Then, after he died, it lay empty for a long time, till that last lady that moved in there, a Mrs Crawford. She started to do it up again. Och, such a sin about her going and dying like that. She was a lovely lady.'

I suddenly warmed to her. 'She was my gran.'

Her face softened. 'Oh, was she really?'

I was already thinking about what she had told me. Perhaps the ghost of that sailor haunted the house. Maybe he materialised in that chair, whenever the sea breezes blew his spirit over the water. 'Did the sailor die in the house?'

She shook her head. 'No, the drunken idiot fell off his boat at Martinique or somewhere like that.'

The image of the ghostly sailor shimmered and was gone from my mind. Now I was puzzled again. 'Did anyone die there, in that house?'

She looked puzzled too. 'What's a young lassie like you doing asking about people dying?'

I didn't have an answer. She came up with one of her own. Surprise, surprise.

Her little face pinched with disapproval. 'Are you trying to put my niece off buying the house?'

I shook my head. 'No, honest, I'm just interested in who used to live there.'

'A saint lived there,' she said at once. 'Long before my time. Sister Kelly she was called. You'll not hear a bad word spoken about her. She's the only one I know died in that house.'

'Why was she such a saint?' I asked.

'She was always helping people. Just out of the goodness of her heart. If anybody needed anything done, Sister Kelly would do it for them. She had an old lady that lived with her. She wasn't even her mother. Sister Kelly took her in and she looked after her anyway. Not many people would do that nowadays.'

'Was she a nurse?' I asked.

'Used to be,' Mrs De Luca said. 'But she was retired when she moved here. Probably in her sixties herself . . . and still taking care of people.' She let out a sigh. 'Aye, she was a good woman. They say she died of a broken heart after the old lady's long-lost relatives came and got her. They found her sitting in an armchair in her bedroom. They hadn't a clue how long she'd been there.' Mrs De Luca's voice became a whisper. 'Couldn't have

49

been a pretty sight. Aye, after all her good works, she died alone. Poor soul.'

I felt the blood drain from my face. They had found her sitting in an armchair, perhaps in the very room I slept in now. No. No perhaps about it. I knew then it *had* been in my room.

Mrs De Luca reached out and touched my hand. 'Did I give you a fright?' She seemed to read my thoughts. 'Don't worry about that woman dying in your house, hen. Sister Kelly was an angel, an angel. She'd never do you any harm.'

11

I walked home in a daze. Someone *had* died in our house. And now, I was sure the ghost of that someone was in my room. Sitting in that chair night after night. Coming closer. But why should I be afraid of such a benevolent ghost? Sister Kelly was an angel, Mrs De Luca said. You don't turn bad when you die. But if you're bad in life, you are equally menacing in death. So, who was this Sister Kelly?

The phone was ringing when I came back in. I hurried to answer it before it woke Aunt Belle. It was my mum. I was so glad to hear her voice.

'Are you having a good time?' she asked.

'Great, Mum. Aunt Belle is so much fun.'

She was worried when I told her Aunt Belle was lying down. 'Is she OK?'

'She's fine. Just a bit of jet lag. I'll tell her you called. And Steven's coming tonight.'

We talked for ages, but I decided not to mention any of my fears. I wanted her and Dad to enjoy themselves, not worry about me. Reluctantly, she rang off, promising to ring again soon.

Aunt Belle got up later, sorry to have missed Mum's call. She seemed better when Steven arrived with Chinese takeaway.

He had news too.

'I'm off tomorrow. I'm going away for a few days with my mates. We've booked a caravan in Blackpool.'

That took me by surprise. 'When did this happen? I thought you were looking forward to a week at home, on your own?'

He strutted about the living room. 'Och well, me and the boys just got it booked at the last minute. You don't mind, do you?'

Aunt Belle shook her head. 'Of course not. You go and have a good time, Steven.'

He came into the kitchen later to help me with the dishes. 'Do you think Aunt Belle's OK? She looks a bit pale.'

'She's fine. She's just a bit tired.'

Steven shrugged. 'It's just you're so cut off from everybody down here. And Mum and Dad are away, and all your friends, and now I'm going. Will you be OK? What if Aunt Belle's sick. She's the one who drives.'

'Yes, and she took lessons at the same driving school as you!'

'Are you complaining about my driving?' It was Aunt Belle at the kitchen door, wearing her lilac silk dressing gown and matching slippers. Now that I really looked at her, she did look pale. But then, she wasn't wearing her wig, and her own hair was sparse and thin, and she had no make-up on and Aunt Belle always wore make-up. Perhaps that was why her face seemed drawn and waxen white.

'Don't listen to her, Aunt Belle,' Steven said. 'She's just jealous 'cause she can't drive.'

I walked him out to his car when he was leaving. 'Are you sure you'll be all right down here?' he said.

'We'll be fine. We're going to have a great time,' I told him.

'I'm probably just being stupid. Trying to be a real big brother for once in my life,' he said. 'I don't know why I'm worried.'

But he was right to be worried.

12

The fifth day

I didn't sleep in the room that night, at least, not while it was dark. I went into Aunt Belle's room and curled up in her armchair and we watched an old Hitchcock film on television. I was asleep before the end and when I woke up it was dawn. Slices of early morning light cut through the clouds. Aunt Belle must have fallen asleep reading. Her book had slipped to the floor and I picked it up and smiled at the title. *Angels of Death*. Trust Aunt Belle, other old ladies are reading nice romantic novels, and my aunt is getting stuck into a murder mystery!

I switched off the TV, went into the kitchen and made myself a cup of tea. And by the time I went back into my room the sun was streaming in through the window. The shadows were all gone. I lay down on the bed and fell asleep.

Aunt Belle was up before me. Aching to get back to

normal. She looked better, showered and dressed in a smart blue dress and jacket, with her make-up and her wig on. 'We're going for a run in the car, honey,' she announced. 'Let's go out for lunch. Is there anywhere round here I can get a decent hamburger?'

We drove to one of the hotels further down the coast and sat on the terrace overlooking the water. From there we could see the island of Arran cloaked in mist.

'You must be fed up with your old auntie, Tyler,' she said over her hamburger (made fresh, chargrilled medium rare, just the way she liked it. I opted for chicken Caesar salad).

'I could never be fed up with you, Aunt Belle,' I assured her.

'I think I'll arrange for that realtor to come tomorrow, to take a look at the house.'

'Realtor?'

'What do you call them here? Estate agents?'

It was late afternoon by the time we got home, and while Aunt Belle called the 'realtor' and arranged for someone to come the next day I tried to text my friends. None of them got through. Their mobiles had either been left at home, or they were in a place where there was no reception. I did miss not being able to talk to them every day. Later, Aunt Belle and I walked along the beach and sat on some rocks to watch the sun sink lower in the sky. It was that beautiful time between dark and light, when the sky is ablaze with colours, orange and purple and topaz. The gloaming, we call it here in Scotland. Such a lovely word.

It had been a perfect day. Aunt Belle seemed almost back to her normal self and there had been no shadows frightening me. While Aunt Belle got ready for bed, I went into the kitchen to make her some hot chocolate. As I waited for the kettle to boil, I stood at the window looking out at the waves crashing up on to the beach. There was something bold and dramatic about this landscape. I would miss this house too when it was sold.

I filled her cup and picked it up, ready to take it into her when I heard a sound in the hall, and a murmured voice. I called out, 'Aunt Belle, is that you?' There was no answer.

I stepped to the kitchen door and gasped. There was an old lady in the hallway. Her white hair was wound in a bun at the top of her head and she was wearing an old-fashioned black coat and carrying a small case.

'Why, my dear, this is lovely,' she said softly. But not to me.

'Excuse me, who are you?' I asked her. She ignored me. She couldn't see me, yet she was as real as I was. I took a step back and when I looked around, the hall was different. There was floral wallpaper, old-fashioned fittings, a claw-footed table of dark wood against the wall. It wasn't our hall at all . . . yet, it *was* our hall.

'I'm so glad you like it, Eleanor,' a kind voice said, a gentle voice. But I couldn't see who that voice belonged to. There was no one else there. No one, but this old lady, Eleanor.

I reached out to touch her, that's how close she was, but my fingers sank into nothing.

Eleanor rubbed at the arm I had tried to touch, and she shivered. 'I suddenly felt cold there,' she said.

The unseen voice said kindly, 'I think there must be a draught somewhere. I'll get it fixed.'

'Oh, no need,' Eleanor said. 'You're being too kind as it is.'

And I knew then I was in the past, watching a scene from another time, just as I had been before when I helped Ben Kincaid. And I knew something else too and the thought chilled me. I knew I was the ghost, not Eleanor, not the unseen voice I could hear. It was me who was the ghost.

But why was I seeing these things? There had to be a reason.

'And this is your room,' the kind voice said. 'I hope you like it.'

The door of my bedroom opened. Someone was there, opening the door. Someone I couldn't see. And now it was no longer my bedroom. There were no green curtains, no tall mirror, no old chest at the bottom of the bed. Everything was white, clean and crisp like snow. Eleanor walked inside and I followed her.

'I just love it,' she said as she laid her case down on the bed. Sister Kelly, you're an angel.'

Eleanor turned and looked straight at me, straight through me. I swung round to see who it was she was talking to. There was no one there. Then, in the blink of an eye, the room was no longer hospital white. It was green and it was mine again, and there was no Eleanor. No invisible Sister Kelly.

And the door slammed shut.

And a shadow shifted in the chair.

13

The sixth day

The cup slipped from my fingers and hot chocolate splashed everywhere. It seemed as if I was moving in slow motion. I wanted to pull at the door, but my hands would not obey me. I could not move. My fingers curled tightly into my palms. Something was sitting there, in that armchair in the corner. Something that meant me harm. And if I stood there long enough, it would come alive, stand up, come towards me.

The door was flung open. Light spilled in from the hallway and Aunt Belle stood there in her lilac dressing gown.

'I'll dehydrate waiting for that hot chocolate.' Then she saw the cup on the floor, her hot chocolate spilled on the carpet. She looked back and saw my face. 'Are you all right, Tyler? What are you doing standing here in the dark?'

I longed to tell her what I had just seen. But even Aunt Belle, with her rich imagination, so like mine, might find it hard to believe. I hardly believed it myself. I managed a smile. 'I only came in for a book, and the door slammed shut again. It scared me to death.'

She slipped her arm in mine. 'Well, let's head out to the light and make some more hot chocolate.'

She led me back into the kitchen, and I glanced back for a second and in the shadow of my room something stirred. I was sure it did.

I spent the rest of the night curled up in the armchair in Aunt Belle's room. She didn't know. Aunt Belle was in a sound sleep well before midnight. When the sun was up, I went back to my own room and fell into an exhausted sleep. I slept soundly too, until Aunt Belle came bustling in with a late morning cup of tea for me. 'The realtor's coming at two,' she said. She felt my brow. 'Are you sure you're not coming down with what I have?'

She always made me smile. 'You think I might have jet lag too?'

'I think I more likely have a virus of some kind . . . I was sick this morning. Maybe that hamburger was off.'

She waved away my worry about that. 'Oh, I'm fine

now. I'm never ill. Not for long. I just don't want to pass anything on to you,' she said.

I swung my legs out of bed. 'Don't worry about me, Aunt Belle. I'm just lazy.'

The 'realtor' was a young woman in a black business suit, wearing heels that were too high and carrying a leather briefcase. Power dressing, I think they call it. We went into the living room and she opened her briefcase and took out her sheaf of papers and I saw how her hands trembled. She was nervous, I thought, probably new to the job.

'Call me Susan,' she insisted as she sat asking questions about the bungalow. Eventually, she stood up. 'I'll just have a look around now, if that's OK?' She began to walk around the room, informing us of all its features as if we didn't know them already. 'A lovely front room, with a bay window. Being on this promontory you're surrounded by the sea. So every room has a sea view. A great selling point. I love the bay windows.' She smiled and opened a cupboard beside the fireplace. 'Ample storage space.' As she spoke she was listing all the house's selling points on the pages on her clipboard. She began walking round from one room to another. Aunt Belle and I followed in her wake. She admired the dining room. 'Could, of course, be a third bedroom.' She was growing more confident as she walked. Her step became a stride. She came to my bedroom and pushed open the door. 'Green,' she said, 'such a relaxing colour.'

If only she knew, I thought. Relaxing was the last thing I would call this room. But I couldn't help but notice how she shivered as we left the room.

From there we moved to Aunt Belle's room. I almost tripped over Aunt Belle's book lying again on the floor. But Susan didn't notice that. She was too busy gushing about the view from the window. Did she too sense the warmth in here? Feel the difference between the two bedrooms?

'And of course, having the en suite in this room is a big plus,' she said.

We ended up in the kitchen. 'Put the kettle on, Tyler. Let's have a cup of tea,' Aunt Belle said.

Susan gushed about the kitchen too, as I suspected she would. It was bright and modern and with doors leading out to a little patio.

It was as we sat having tea that Susan, checking her housing schedule, realised something she had almost missed. 'Oh, wait a minute . . . there's a cellar in this house.'

'Do you know, I forgot all about that,' Aunt Belle said. She stood up. 'It's in the hall, Tyler. Almost below your room. No wonder it's cold. The draught is probably coming up from there. Fancy me forgetting we had a cellar.'

We all went into the hall. 'It's supposed to be just here,' Susan said. 'May I?' She moved aside a rug on the floor just outside my room.

No one would have known there was a hatch there. The handle folded in flush against the floor. It took a few pulls to lift it free.

A gust of cold air hit us. I stepped back.

There were steps that descended into darkness. Susan went down first. 'Have you got a flashlight?'

'Oh, there's electricity. There's a switch somewhere.' And, with that, Aunt Belle was off down the stairs. I stood at the top, didn't fancy going down into that dark place.

'I remember we were so excited when we found this,' Aunt Belle went on. 'Thought it could be a wine cellar, or we could store food in it.'

Aunt Belle found the switch and the cellar lit up. I had expected the cellar to be damp and dirty, but it wasn't. It was a bright, white square room.

'It is a good size,' Susan said. 'Yes, a great feature. It could be used as a games room or a den.'

She continued talking but her voice began to fade. And it seemed then that I was in another place, another time. Aunt Belle and Susan seemed to be moving in slow motion. It was as if there was a veil between them and me. The cellar was no longer bright and white and clean. It was the way it once must have been – dark and damp and full of shadows. Moving shadows.

My heart pounded at my chest. I had to get out of here. I took a step back and turned.

And I was looking right into watery blue eyes and an old wrinkled face, skin like a withered apple, close to my own. Too close. It was the old lady, it was Eleanor's face, but changed so much I hardly recognised her. Her white hair was wild and loose about her shoulders and her eyes looked terrified. She was so close. Her hand touched my shoulder, turned it to ice. Her breath was grave cold against my ear.

'Help me, Tyler,' she whispered.

And I screamed.

14

'Tyler, Tyler,' said a voice. It sounded as if it was coming towards me down a long tunnel. 'Tyler.'

I was afraid to open my eyes. Afraid of what I might see.

'Tyler! Tyler, honey!' I opened my eyes at last. Aunt Belle's worried face broke into a relieved smile. 'Oh, honey, you gave me such a scare.'

I was still in the cellar, but now it was light and bright again. 'If I hadn't caught you, you would have gone down the whole flight of stairs,' she said. Now that I seemed to be fine, Aunt Belle could even see the funny side. 'Lucky I've got a bit of fat on me. I broke your fall.' Then she hugged me.

I wanted to tell her, I longed to tell her, about the face, the shadow in my room, the cold. If Susan hadn't been there, I'm sure I would have told her right at that moment. But then Susan's face appeared behind my aunt.

'Let's get you back upstairs,' she said. 'You just lost your footing. Easy to do on these steep steps.'

When we reached the hall Susan asked, 'Do you want to lie down?' She indicated my room.

'No!' I almost shouted it. My room was the last place I wanted to be. 'No, I'll be fine in the front room.'

They must have wondered why. I saw them exchange glances, but they didn't say anything. But I couldn't bear the thought of going in there, in case that old woman was waiting there for me too.

I limped into the front room and Aunt Belle went off to the kitchen to make more tea. Aunt Belle's answer to everything.

'It's a lovely little house,' Susan said, dropping back into estate agent mode for want of anything else to say. 'It really will be easy to sell.'

'Were you the one who rented it out to the last people?' I asked her.

'The Forbes? Yes, I was.'

'They left because of his job, didn't they?'

She didn't answer straight away. Maybe she was just

writing something on her clipboard, but I didn't think so. She was thinking about what to say. 'Yes,' she said. 'Funny though, they rented another house not a mile from here. Up on the hill.'

'They're still here? In the village?'

She turned to me then. 'Yes, up on Craigview Drive. They rented a semi-detached house up there. Nice, but not half as nice as this.'

Now I was puzzled. Why did they leave so suddenly and move only a mile from here? Had something scared them too?

It was just as Susan was leaving that Aunt Belle was sick. Her face went suddenly pale and she ran into the bathroom. I hurried in after her. 'What's wrong?'

She splashed her face with water. 'I don't know. It just came over me.' She smiled at Susan, who was standing in the doorway looking concerned. 'It's Tyler here, I think she's trying to poison me. She's my sole heir. She gets this house if anything happens to me.'

Not used to Aunt Belle's sense of humour, Susan looked a bit taken aback.

'Don't worry,' I said to Susan, 'your tea was OK. I only poison one person a day.'

We giggled as we watched Susan drive off. 'Poor soul,' Aunt Belle said. 'You'd better take good care of me, or she'll be having you arrested.'

Then she ran into the bathroom again and was sick. 'I think I'll lie down,' she said as I lead her back into her bedroom. 'I got quite a shock there in the cellar. When I saw you just about to tumble down those stairs, my stomach did a somersault too.'

She lay down on her bed. 'Maybe you can go and get me some fruit. Some oranges maybe.'

'Sure I will. As long as you'll be fine on your own.'

'Feel better already,' she said. But she lied. I picked up her book and put it on her bedside table.

'Here's your book if you want to read.'

I had planned to tell her all about the things that had happened to me. I had promised myself I would tell her after Susan left. But how could I do it now, when her face was so pale and she looked so tired?

'I think I just need a nap,' she said.

She was sound asleep by the time I left the house. I wasn't really wary of leaving her by herself. Somehow I knew she was safe in her own bedroom. It was me the ghosts wanted to reach . . . But now I had another thought. Maybe they had tried to reach someone else

68

too. Perhaps the Forbes family had also experienced strange things.

I had to meet them, talk to them. Find out the reason they had left so suddenly.

15

Craigview Drive was situated high on the hill over-looking the village. It only had four houses on it. It was easy finding the one the Forbes were renting. A woman opened the door. A redhead. She looked as if she was sucking something sour. 'Yes?' She didn't smile.

'Hello, my name is Tyler Lawless . . . My aunt owns Mille Failte.'

Did she catch her breath when I mentioned the name of the house? I was sure she did, but her face stayed as tight as ever.

I had a story ready and began to blurt it out before she could shut the door on me. I had found something in the house, I said, and I wanted to check if it belonged to any of her family. I had a soft leather purse in my hand, one of my old ones.

I held it out to her as I told her my story. I had hoped she would invite me in so I could get talking to her. But by the grim expression on her face as she took the purse from me and turned it over in her hand, I doubted that now.

'Never seen this before,' she said, and she handed it back to me. She managed a muttered sorry before she began to close the door on me. I couldn't let her do that. I decided to be honest with her.

'Please, that's not the real reason I came here.' I held out the purse. 'I know this doesn't belong to you.' The door was almost closed.

'So why *are* you here?'

'I need to know why you didn't stay in Mille Failte. Why you left so suddenly.'

Her eyes flashed angrily and she sucked in her cheeks. 'We left because of my husband's job.'

I wasn't going to accept that. 'You've only moved a few streets away. That's not the truth.'

'Are you calling me a liar?'

I was getting her back up. I took a step closer, afraid, this time, she would shut the door in my face.

'It's actually none of your business why we left. I didn't like the house. All right?'

71

'I'm living there now. I need to know if something happened in that house. Something weird.'

That shot home. She couldn't hide the sudden flash of understanding in her eyes. For a second I thought it might make a difference, but I was wrong. 'Good luck,' was all she said.

She was about to shut the door so I splayed my hand against the wood, holding it open. 'Why would I need good luck?'

I thought again she was going to tell me something, say something more. She stared at me for a long moment. Giving herself time to think. Then she glanced back into the house. She'd made a decision. 'I have to go. I have something on the hob.' And a second later, I was staring at a closed door.

I stood for a moment, not quite knowing what to do. If I knocked again, she would ignore me, somehow I knew that. Was she even now standing in her hallway, watching the door, praying for me to go away? I imagined I could see her through the wood and glass, willing me to leave. She was afraid. Couldn't she see I was afraid too? Why couldn't she tell me what she was afraid of? What harm could come to her now? So far away from Mille Failte?

I walked down the path to the street, and began to go back down the hill. The view from up here was wonderful. I stood for a moment and watched the long line of surf crashing against the rocks, a pale misty sun sending a gold shimmer over the river. Coming here to see the Forbes had been a waste of time. I was no closer to the truth.

I didn't hear the footsteps coming fast behind me. The hand on my shoulder made me jump.

It was a boy, my own age, his light brown hair falling carelessly over his brow. And I could see the resemblance to the woman I had just been talking to, except that he had a smile in his brown eyes.

'I'm Paul Forbes.' He glanced back to his house, pulled me in towards the bushes. As if she might be watching us. 'My mother won't talk to you. You've got to understand why.'

'Understand what? Why won't she tell me why you left the house so suddenly?'

'Because she's scared. We've been out of that house for months, and she's still afraid.'

'Afraid of . . . what?'

'The same thing you're afraid of. Something's happening to you, isn't it?' he asked.

Saying it now, in the open, to someone almost made me cry. Telling someone at last. 'There's something in that house. I don't know what. You're the only people I can think of to talk to. I need to know what made you leave.'

'I'm not sure if I can help you,' Paul Forbes said. 'Couldn't even help myself when we lived there. But I will tell you everything that happened to us.'

16

There was an old wooden bus shelter on the tree-lined road that wound down to the shore. We sat in there to talk. And there, out of the sun, in the shadows, Paul began to tell me his story.

'Right from the first night, I knew there was something in that house,' he said. 'In that bedroom.'

I didn't need to ask which bedroom. I knew.

He went on. 'It was the cold at first. Do you feel that too?'

'Yes, the rest of the house is fine, but that one room . . .'

He nodded. 'And the chair in the corner?'

Just thinking of it, even on this warm afternoon, chilled me. 'In the dark it looks as if someone's sitting there,' I said.

'It freaked me out,' Paul said, I tried to tell my dad but he wouldn't believe me.' He smiled. 'The only books I read are about zombies and vampires. So my dad, and my mum, thought I was letting my imagination run away with me.'

'That's what they always say about me too.' And I told him my name and about how I was staying with Aunt Belle, and about Mum and Dad being away in Australia. 'There's no one I can talk to about this.' I felt my voice catch in my throat at the sudden realisation of how alone I was. Isolated.

'You can talk to me, Tyler,' he said.

So I began to tell him how the shadow was haunting me too, every night in that room. He didn't know about the cellar, but he did know about Sister Kelly.

'Sister Kelly,' I said. 'She was almost a saint, so I've heard. Looked after an old lady.'

'Did you know the old lady tried to escape?' Paul said.

'Escape? What do you mean?'

He shook his head. 'The woman at The Delicatessen told me. She knows everything. Of course, she didn't call it an escape. According to her, the old woman had dementia, went wandering. When the police found her, she said she'd been kidnapped, was being kept prisoner. And do you know what they did?'

I was sure I did know. 'They took her straight back to Sister Kelly.'

'Yes, they didn't believe her, because she didn't know what she was saying, poor old soul, and Sister Kelly was an angel looking after her, they said. But I began to wonder . . . Maybe the old lady was telling the truth. Maybe this Sister Kelly wasn't the angel she was made out to be.'

I hesitated to go on. 'I've seen that old lady.' I saw her again in my mind's eye, there in the cellar. Terrified.

He shot forward. 'You've got to be kidding.'

'She's called Eleanor. I've seen her twice. The first time she looked so happy, but the second time . . .' I flinched at the memory of it. 'It was in that cellar. She was terrified. She asked me to help her.'

'Help her . . . ? If she's dead, how are you supposed to help her?'

How could I tell him about Ben Kincaid? I daren't lose his trust now. So I only said, 'I don't know.'

'Is she the shadow in the chair? This Eleanor?'

And I knew right then she wasn't. 'No,' I told him. 'There's something vulnerable about her. Not sinister at all. Sister Kelly was the one they found dead in a chair in that room. And I think she's still there in that room.'

'Wow! You're having it worse than I did, Tyler.'

'So what in the end made you leave?' I asked him.

'I was scared stiff of that . . . thing . . . that . . . ' He hesitated, not knowing what to call it. 'That shadow. I'd sleep with the light on, and the light would be off again when I woke up. Dad said it was a bulb that had gone. He always had a reasonable explanation.'

'And the door that wouldn't stay open?'

'Subsidence.' We said it at the same time.

Paul took a deep breath, as if the next bit still terrified him. 'Then one night, I fell asleep and I dreamed. I dreamed of spiders, hundreds of them were crawling all over the bed, and I was suddenly wide awake and the room was pitch-black and it was there, that shadow standing right beside my bed. I've never screamed in my life but I screamed then. I was out of that room so fast, and even though my dad was sick he came running out to me and I was pure shaking with terror. Couldn't stop.'

He took a deep breath. 'Mum said I'd been dreaming. That's all it was, she said, just a nightmare. I told them I was never sleeping in that room again, and I didn't. But the next night, my mum did.'

It was a moment before he went on. 'I tried to stop her, but she was convinced nothing would happen to her. She wanted me to see there was nothing to be scared of. I stayed awake all night. I just sat in that front room praying I was wrong. And then, about three in the morning she started screaming.'

Paul paused, but when he spoke again it came out in one unbroken stream of words. 'I'd never heard such screaming. Me and my dad tried to get the door of the room open but it wouldn't budge, and Dad had to break it down. My mum was lying on her back on the bed, her eyes wide open, just staring, and me and Dad carried her into the front room. My dad was ready to call an ambulance, but my mum got really panicky when he said that, and she started yelling, "We're getting out of here. That thing wants us out of here."'

He took another long deep breath. 'That's what she said. "That thing wants us out of here." The next day we went to a hotel. I've tried to ask Mum about it, about what happened, but she won't talk about it. Now, she says it was just her imagination. Didn't really happen at all. That's why she was rude to you. She pretends it never happened.'

He sighed. 'I began to think, to hope, it was just my imagination as well, until I heard you talking to Mum.'

'What did you mean when you said . . . about your dad being sick? Is your dad ill?'

'Not any more. We don't know what was wrong with

him, but once we were out of that house, he made a complete recovery. Why?'

'Because, my aunt Belle, she's sick too. I thought it was jet lag – she's just arrived from the States – or that maybe she'd picked up a virus. But now . . .'

'It's that house, Tyler. That house is making her ill.'

'What am I going to do?'

'Get out of that house, Tyler. Take your aunt and go back home. I don't know what's in there. But I really believe it's something evil.'

17

Get out of that house. Good advice. I wished I could take it. But how could I explain that to Aunt Belle? She had sensed nothing and loved the place. She wanted a good price for it. She wouldn't even get it sold if people thought it was haunted. There was no way I could leave Mille Failte. Not for the moment anyway.

Aunt Belle was still asleep when I went back. Her room was bathed in golden light. The window was open and her curtains fluttered in the early evening breeze. I could hear the seagulls cawing as they flew over the beach. Why was it that this room was always welcoming and safe? Why was it only the bedroom I slept in that held such ominous menace? I answered the question myself. Sister Kelly, the saintly Sister Kelly, had died there.

I remembered Paul's words, what his mum had said, *That thing wants us out of here*. Something was trying to scare us away too.

But something else was keeping me here. Could that something be the ghost of Eleanor?

I sat curled up in the chair and watched Aunt Belle as she slept. When I felt her brow, she felt cool to the touch, but she must have been awake at some time and read her book for it had slipped on to the floor again. I was afraid it wasn't just jet lag she had. Or even a bug. What if it *was* this house that was making her ill? What if there was something really wrong with her?

Sitting there, watching her, I felt once again so alone. And I was so afraid.

Something evil was here, oozing through the walls, coming up through the floor. From the cellar.

I shivered, remembering that wrinkled, frightened face and those whispered words. *Help me, Tyler*. And though it was the last thing I wanted to do, I found myself standing up, and my feet began leading me out of my aunt's room. I stopped at the door, looked down the hallway.

And the hatch to the cellar was lying open.

* * *

82

It hadn't been open when I came home. I had walked through the hall into the kitchen, and the hatch had been closed. The rug had been lying over it. Yet, now here it was, open, luring me down. I couldn't stop heading towards it. Step by step. Closer and closer. With every step I grew colder. I wanted to stop but it was as if I had no control over my body, almost as if I was being drawn towards the gaping hole.

And then I was at the top, staring down into that desolate darkness.

Something was moving down there. Shadows, moving, as if something was waiting for me. And I could hear whispers too. Whispers winding their way up through the darkness towards me. Whispers I couldn't make out, and didn't want to. Even so, I put one foot on the top step. I tried desperately to stop myself from taking another step, knowing I was powerless.

'She's coming . . .' I heard those whispered words and my breath caught in my throat. I was sure that was what I heard, a fluttering of whispers. 'She's coming.'

Down there, something was waiting for me.

'Tyler!'

I stepped back and at that same second the hatch

slammed closed almost on my legs. 'Tyler!' my aunt's voice called out, saving me.

My head throbbed. My heart raced. It felt like for ever before I could move.

'Tyler, are you there, honey?'

'I'm here, Aunt Belle. I'm coming.' And I ran into her room.

Aunt Belle didn't want to eat any tea that evening – afraid she might be sick again. She assured me it was only a bug she had. Nothing to worry about.

'You pick up so much on these long transatlantic flights. Can you imagine all those people's germs floating around the cabin, looking for someone to land on? And that someone is always me. I always said I was irresistible!'

That made me smile, but I was still worried about her. I wanted to call the doctor in the morning. She was determined I shouldn't do that.

'A doctor? At my age? He'll whip me into hospital, before you can say "senior citizen", and then I really will be ill. I keep well away from doctors, Tyler.'

A visit to the pharmacist was the most she would permit.

I spent the evening curled up in her chair, watching

TV. The only time I ventured out of her room was to fill a fresh jug of water for her. And I couldn't keep my eyes from wandering to that hatch in the hall.

Be brave, Tyler, I told myself, drawing my courage around me like a cloak. *You're being kept here for a purpose. You have to find out what it is.*

I stood at the kitchen door, watching, waiting, angry with myself for letting all this get to me. Finally, I came to a decision. At least there was something I could do about the cellar. There was a heavy chest of drawers against the wall in the hallway. I hauled at it with every bit of strength I had and dragged it till it sat square on top of the hatch.

There! I thought. *Let anything lift it now.*

18

The seventh day

Early in the morning, before Aunt Belle was awake, I was in the shower. I dressed and headed for the village store. The wonderful smell of baking wafted towards me as I walked in. I would bring back fresh rolls and milk to brighten my aunt's day.

The shop had only just opened. A couple of workmen were in front of me buying papers, and waiting for rolls to be buttered and filled with bacon for them. Finally, it was my turn. Mrs De Luca, behind the counter, obviously recognised me. Her face screwed up in a frown. 'How's your auntie?' she asked, as if she cared. 'Did the wee tonic I gave you help her?'

'Didn't seem to. I think she's got a bug.'

'You should get her to a doctor,' she said.

'She doesn't like doctors,' I replied. 'I thought I might get her some fruit.'

'She's quite right about doctors. I don't trust any of them. As long as she gets plenty of fluid, she'll be fine,' she said.

Now that she had taken on the role of our private medical consultant I dared ask her about Eleanor. 'Someone was telling me that the old lady who used to live in our house ran away from that Sister Kelly?'

She looked suspicious. 'Ran away?'

I shrugged. '*Did* the old lady try to escape?'

'Escape? Where do you think she was, Colditz? The poor soul's mind was gone. She just wandered away. She was all mixed up, didn't know what she was saying. It wasn't long after that her relatives came and got her. She was bedridden by that time.'

'Are you sure the relatives came and took her away? She didn't die in the house?'

She snapped an answer at me. 'What is it with you and this dying! The only one that died there was poor Sister Kelly! Died of a broken heart when the old lady was taken away from her.'

I thought about Sister Kelly all the way home. The 'saintly' woman. The gentle voice I had first heard telling Eleanor, 'This is your home now.' But who was she really? And what had happened here?

*   *   *

Aunt Belle ate the rolls hungrily. I could see she so wanted to be better. Then she took her vitamin tonic. Two spoonfuls. But she was happy to stay in bed and watch television.

'One more day,' I told her. 'If you're not feeling better tomorrow, I'm phoning a doctor. Only for advice. Don't worry I won't let anybody drag you off to hospital.'

She waved me away with her scarlet-nailed hand and I saw that her polish was cracked. Aunt Belle would normally never let that happen. I think that worried me more than anything else.

Mum phoned that morning too. They were having a wonderful time. They were in Brisbane, getting ready for a trip up the Gold Coast. Her and Dad were missing me, worrying about me. Was everything OK?

'Everything's great,' I assured her. She was a bit worried when I told her about Steven going on holiday with his mates and she called the news out to Dad and my uncle, who were firing up the barbie. I heard my dad call back, 'He'll be fine. Stop fussing.'

This time she had a long chat with Aunt Belle too. And I could hear her laughing on the other side of the world.

Aunt Belle had said nothing about not feeling well, so

neither would I. Instead I told Mum about having the estate agent in. Then, I had a brainwave. Maybe Mum knew something about this house.

'We've been trying to find out about the history of the house. The lady at the village shop mentioned someone called Sister Kelly, who used to live here.'

'Not you too,' Mum said.

I held my breath. 'What do you mean?'

'That Sister Kelly, your gran was trying to find out about her too. I remember her talking about her. I think she said she died in that house . . . but don't tell Aunt Belle that, whatever you do!' I heard Dad calling for her. 'I have to go, Tyler. I'm not pulling my weight here. They won't feed me if I don't do some work!'

I stood by the phone after she'd gone, my mind in a whirl. *This house has a history*, Gran had written in her letter. She had been interested in Sister Kelly too. And if my gran had tried to find out more about this woman . . . then so would I.

19

After the phone call Aunt Belle was determined to get back to normal. She had a bath, put on her make-up and her wig, and appeared in the kitchen looking just like the Aunt Belle I knew and loved. Except for her nails. She held them out to me.

'Chipped nails. I can't bear chipped nails. You have to help me, Tyler.' She pleaded as if it was life or death to her, so after lunch I sat with her hand in mine and painted her nails.

When I was finished, she held out her hands, with rings on her long slim fingers. 'My goodness, Aunt Belle, you're more glamorous than I could ever be.'

She didn't even deny it. 'We'll soon change that,' she said. 'I'll do your nails next.'

She painted them with a dark blue polish she was sure I would love. I couldn't help but notice how her hand trembled just a little. My heart sank. She was putting on a brave face, wanting so much to be well, trying to make me feel better too.

'We can stay in today,' I said. 'It's a lovely day, we can sit on the patio, get some sun.'

She was having none of that. 'I've had enough nice days in. I need a day out.'

We decided to walk along the beach, drink in that invigorating sea air and go for an early dinner at the steakhouse at the far end of the shore. If Aunt Belle didn't feel like the walk back, we would call for a taxi.

While she got herself ready, I made her bed. I picked her book up from the floor again and tidied her dressing table. I smiled at the number of creams and lotions she had.

'That's why I look so young,' she once told me. 'You know, my doctor says I have the body of a twenty-year-old.'

Gran had been there at the time and she had answered her so quickly I fell about laughing. 'Well, I think it's time the twenty-year-old got it back,' she had said.

The memory of that day made me want to cry. I sat on the chair, next to the bed and remembered my gran. *What's happening, Gran?* I thought, praying to her silently. *I wish you could help me. You knew something, I just know you did.*

I closed my eyes and I felt her warm presence all around me. I was sure if I opened them she would be there, standing in front of me, smiling, telling me all I needed to know.

'Tyler? Are you ready?' I opened my eyes and there she was. Aunt Belle, so like my gran that just for a second I could have sworn it was her.

'I thought you were having a nap,' Aunt Belle said.

She took my arm as we walked the length of the beach, stopping now and then to watch the tide come in. I could see the tiredness etched in her face by the time we had reached the restaurant. She didn't have the steak. And she pushed the salad she had ordered around her plate, but ate little of it.

'I'm spoiling your summer, honey,' she said. 'I'm sorry.'

'Aunt Belle, I'm having a lovely time. I just want you to feel better. Maybe,' I ventured, 'we should go to a hotel. Stay there? All your meals made for you, room service every day . . .'

She looked at me as if I had just gone crazy. 'A hotel! And leave our lovely little house. What on earth are you suggesting that for, Tyler? I wouldn't leave there for the world. It's my last tie with your gran. I want to stay there till I see it sold.'

And that was the end of it. We would have to stay there. Nothing was going to convince her to leave.

'I'm sure I'll be OK tomorrow,' she said confidently.

Always tomorrow, I thought.

We took a taxi home, and she was back in bed half an hour after we stepped inside the house. I went into the kitchen to make her some hot chocolate. On my way, I checked the chest of drawers was still firmly in place on top of the hatch. I had no intention of sleeping in that room, but I would have to go in there to get some fresh pyjamas. It seemed sensible to go in there while it was still light and I was waiting for the kettle to boil. I could hear Aunt Belle's TV. She was watching an old episode of *Star Trek* and the sound of her programme reassured me that there was nothing to fear in here. Not with the setting sun sending rays of orange twilight into the house.

Yet, I felt as if I was stepping into another world, venturing into the unknown. I took a deep breath, it would only take a moment, I told myself. I would be in and out in seconds.

The cold wrapped itself around me. I pulled open the drawer where my pyjamas were kept, promising myself that the rest of my clothes were coming out of here tomorrow.

And in the blink of an eye it happened. One second I was bending over the drawer, and the next the door of the room had closed. There was no twilight in here any more, only darkness. The room had changed too. The bed was no longer my modern divan, but an old iron bedstead with brass knobs. No duvet, just a thin woven spread.

And I wasn't alone.

Eleanor was there. She looked just the way she had when I had seen her in the cellar. Her grey hair was falling untidily on her shoulders. Her thin dress was worn and stained. She was hitting against the door with frail fingers. 'Please . . . Let me out . . . Oh, please.'

I got to my feet and as I moved she swung round, seemed to lose her footing and stumble against the wall. Without thinking, I reached out to help her. Her eyes grew wild and she screamed. I knew she could see me, and to her I was a ghost.

She sank to the floor. 'Let me out! Please. Let me out!' Her eyes never left me. 'This room's haunted, I tell you. There's a ghost in here.'

I reached out again. 'I won't hurt you.' My voice was like a far whisper, a sound from another time. 'I want to help.'

But she was just too scared. She shifted back against the door and began scratching at it again with her nails. 'Let me out . . .'

And then I heard another voice. The same voice I had heard before. But now with no gentleness or kindness in it. Sister Kelly. 'Shut your old moaning face. If I'd known you would be this much trouble, I'd never have taken you in.'

The voice scared me. There was so much cruelty in it. Eleanor began to cry softly. I wanted so much to help her. Drag her back to my time. To safety. But when I reached out again, my hands only passed through air. 'I want to help you,' I said again softly.

Could she hear me? I don't know, but her eyes seemed to clear, as if she suddenly recognised me, and her voice shook. 'Help me, Tyler. Please, help me.'

And then, she was gone.

20

The eighth day

Eleanor had come back, appeared once again, to let me see what had happened to her. To make sure I stayed. She wanted me here, wanted me to help her. But how was I meant to do that?

I had changed the past before, but how was I supposed to do it again!

I sat by Aunt Belle's bed until darkness fell. I so needed someone to confide in and I thought about Paul Forbes. He had been afraid too. I could tell him, talk to him. But I had no number to call him. The only way I could get in touch with him was to go back to his house, and I knew I was probably the last person his mother wanted to see.

'Don't you sleep in here with me,' was the last thing Aunt Belle said to me before she drifted off to sleep. 'You get into your own bed. Get a good night's sleep.'

A good night's sleep was the last thing I could get in my own room.

'I'm not going to die tonight,' she said, and she laughed. But if she could see herself. So frail-looking without her wig, without her make-up.

'I'm going to call the doctor tomorrow,' I said.

I did sleep in her room that night, though she wasn't aware of it, deep in sleep long before me. But I felt safe in here with her. Nothing could reach me here. Even in darkness, there were no menacing shadows.

The next day shone bright and clear, if a little cold. I left Aunt Belle sitting up in bed, watching television. I promised her I would be back shortly. I was going to the chemist, I told her, and it wasn't a lie. I would go to the chemist, but before that, I took the long winding road from the shore up the hill to Paul Forbes's house.

I had to gather my strength to knock at the door and I prayed Mrs Forbes wasn't going to be the one who opened it.

My prayers weren't answered. She looked angry when she saw me.

'You again. What do you want?'

'Something's happening to me in that house. I know it happened to you too.'

'Who told you something happened to me?'

I tried to look behind her. 'Is Paul in?'

She pushed the door further closed. Held it. 'How do you know Paul? What do you want with him?' She wanted me away. One more second the door would be closed in my face. 'Leave us alone. But I'll give you one bit of advice. Get out of that house.'

I wanted to explain to her that I couldn't, but she had already slammed the door in anger.

I stood for a moment, and I heard raised voices from inside the house. I stopped, because one of those voices was Paul's. A moment later the door was hauled open again and Paul was there, his hair ruffled. He was wearing a T-shirt and shorts that looked as if he'd slept in them.

'I don't want you involved in this, Paul!' his mother shouted from inside the house. 'That girl's trouble. I just know it.'

'Give me five minutes, Mum,' Paul called back.

He pulled the door closed behind him. 'Has something else happened? he asked.

'I've seen Eleanor again. Sister Kelly did keep her

prisoner. I heard her voice. Only this time, it was different. It sounded so cruel, Paul.'

'My mum's right, you know. You should get out of that house.'

'My aunt won't leave.' I sat on his wall, aware of his mother's grim eyes watching us from the window. 'And I can't leave either. I think that . . .' I hesitated to say what I felt was the truth. 'I think that Eleanor is keeping me there.'

He sat on the wall across from me. 'I don't understand.'

'I think you're right. There's something that wants me out, the way it wanted you out – that something evil you talked about . . . it's trying to scare me away. But there's something else that wants me to stay. I think that something is Eleanor. I think I'm supposed to be there. For a purpose.'

Now he was even more puzzled. 'For a purpose?'

'I think I'm here to help the old lady. Eleanor.'

'You said that before, but . . . help her? She's long dead. How can you help her?'

Could I tell him, I wondered. Confide in him. Tell him something so unbelievable. 'I think maybe I'm meant to stop her from dying. Save her from Sister Kelly.'

I carried on quickly. If I stopped now, I would never have the courage to go on. 'Please listen to me, Paul. I promise you I'm telling the truth about this. I know I can save her. I've done it before. There was a boy in my school, Ben Kincaid. He'd died a long time ago. I kept seeing his ghost, and he kept asking me to help him. I couldn't understand how, or why. And I was so scared.' And I told him everything about what happened with Ben Kincaid. I saw his face change. I was sure he was going to get up and walk away and I had to keep him there. 'I know it sounds totally unbelievable, but it's true. It happened. I went back in time and changed the past.'

Paul was still watching me, saying nothing. 'And there's something else you have to understand. To save Eleanor I'll have to change the past again, and everything will be different. If I save her, then there won't be any ghost in the house, so your family won't have been forced to leave, and I'll never have met you. You won't remember any of this, because it never happened.'

How unbelievable it all sounded. If I was Paul, I would think it was all nonsense.

But I was surprised by his reaction. His face broke into a smile. 'You can really do that?' He beamed. 'Cool trick.'

'So, you see, I have to stay. That's what I'm here for.'

He was quiet for a moment. 'Give me your phone.' He held out his hand. 'I should have given you this the last time I saw you.' I handed over my phone and he keyed in his number for me. Then he glanced back at the house. His mother was still at the window, peering through the venetian blinds.

'I better go. But remember, you can call me anytime. Day or night. I mean that.'

I felt better after speaking to Paul, and now, knowing his mobile number, I felt at least I had someone I could talk to. Someone who believed me.

21

The chemist was at the far end of the main street. I told her my aunt's symptoms and she seemed to think Aunt Belle was right. It was probably just a bug she had picked up on the plane. I so wanted that to be the case I didn't even question it. 'But if there is no improvement by tomorrow, call the doctor. No matter what she says,' she told me. 'At her age you can't take any chances.'

Aunt Belle was sleeping when I got back in the house. But it looked as if she'd been up. Looking for her book again by the way books were scattered across the floor. Her own book was the first one I picked up. *Angels of Death*.

I held it in my hand and began to think. How often had I picked this book up from the floor? I'd lost count. *Angels of Death*. Always there on the floor waiting for me.

Waiting.

Now why should I use that word?

And it wasn't a murder mystery as I had first thought, but real-life case histories of unsolved murders. I opened the book, and there written in her neat hand, was my gran's name. Rosina Tyler Crawford. She always wrote her name in her books. This wasn't Aunt Belle's book at all. It was my gran's. I turned to the title page.

ANGELS OF DEATH

Nurses Who Kill

I sat on the floor and began to flick through the pages. This book wasn't just about unsolved murders. It was about murders by nurses, by doctors, by carers. Chapter after chapter told stories of people in the medical profession who had abused the trust placed in them. This was my gran's book. A message from the other side, meant for me to find. She was trying to pass information on to me. I looked around this room, always so warm and welcoming, and I knew then, without seeing her, that my gran was present here. She was in this room, watching over me and Aunt Belle. It was Gran who had made sure I would find this book, though it had taken me ages to figure that out.

'I won't let you down now, Gran,' I whispered. And as if in answer a breeze came in from the window and the curtains fluttered.

I looked back to the book. One of the pages was bookmarked. I opened it.

CHAPTER 10
The Missing Murderess

And that's when I saw that it wasn't a bookmark in the page at all. It was a photograph. A photograph of a tall woman with dark hair. Her hand was raised, as if she was trying to cover her face, as if she wanted to hide it from the camera. As if she didn't want to be photographed at all. And she was standing at the front door of this bungalow. I recognised the honeysuckle and the sign. *Mille Failte*. I turned the photograph over and there, written in my gran's fine hand, was a name.

Sister Kelly

And a question.

The missing murderess?

22

I took a deep breath and began to read the chapter.

In the early years of the First World War, a young nurse, Mary Duff, worked with wounded soldiers in Italy. She was popular with soldiers and staff alike, always willing to work extra hours, a nurse who would never leave the side of a dying soldier. Then it began to be noticed that the soldiers she remained with usually did die, even when they were expected to survive. She was always on hand when there was an emergency and it seemed there were more emergencies on her shift than anyone else's.

But soldiers die all the time in the theatre of war so no great notice was taken of it until one young soldier who was brought in refused to be treated by her. The Angel of Death, he called her. No one listened to him. He was considered delirious. That night, on her shift, the young soldier suffered a massive trauma and died. Though nothing could be proved against her, Nurse Mary Duff was sent home. And seemed to disappear . . . or did she?

1925. A veteran's hospital in Florida, and another spate of unexplained deaths, and always when Sister Catherine Macey was on the ward. But Catherine Macey was a saint, everyone said so. A nurse who spent long hours on the ward tending her patients. But was she in fact, Mary Duff? The ages certainly match. Catherine Macey was almost thirty, the same age Mary Duff would have been. It took another two years, and many unexplained deaths in the hospital before Catherine Macey was forced to resign.

She seemed to disappear too. But did she resurface in a Cincinatti hospital in 1933? The caring Dorothy Blake. Another saint. But once again, patients started dying who had been expected to live. Then, just as investigations about her began, Dorothy Blake resigned and moved on.

Did she move to New York? In 1944 there were more unexplained deaths on the watch of Sister Margaret Campbell, and was this Margaret Campbell also Mary Cameron, who worked at an old people's home in England in the 1950s?

There is no concrete evidence. The only photograph of any of these women that exists is a blurred photograph of Dorothy Blake taken at a party at the hospital where she worked.

Where did these women go? Or are they all the same woman? And what happened to her after Mary Cameron disappeared? Did she die? Or did she continue her catalogue of killing under yet another identity?

I looked back at the photograph in my hand. Sister Kelly trying to turn her face from the camera, reluctant to have her photo taken at all. Could anyone be this evil? And just how many deaths had all these women been responsible for? In each case, this nurse was at first considered a heroine, a saint, just like Sister Kelly, when in fact she had been something else . . . something evil.

I had to find out more.

I went into the living room and powered up my laptop. I keyed in each of the names in turn, from Mary Duff to Mary Cameron, and read all the information there was about each of them. The same facts emerged time after time.

And then, just when I thought I had exhausted everything, I came across the photograph mentioned in Gran's book. The one of Dorothy Blake taken at a party. You could hardly make her out, her face was so blurred. She was standing at the back, her hand once again reaching up to cover her face, but the camera had been too quick for her. I stared at the screen, looking from the photograph there, to the other, taken outside this house, trying to see a resemblance.

I clicked to enlarge the image. And as I peered closer I thought, surely this had to be the same person? Same dark hair, same features, same face. It had to be her.

I maximised the image even further, so that the screen was filled with that face. 'Yes,' I said aloud. 'You *are* Sister Kelly.'

And as I spoke her name I heard a roar, a sound that seemed to come from the depths of darkness.

And I screamed in terror.

23

Next thing I knew Aunt Belle was hurrying into the living room. 'I heard you scream. What on earth happened?'

I so wanted to tell her. To share my fear with someone. But not her, not now. I had to think fast.

'I . . . I got an electric shock off the computer.' My voice trembled.

She was all concern. 'Switch that thing off. Unplug it.' She was looking around for the cable.

'I'll do it, Aunt Belle.' I was happy to do it. I snapped the laptop shut and took it into my room. I didn't even step over the threshold, just stood at the door and threw it on the bed. Then I slammed the door closed and went back into the living room. Aunt Belle was sitting in one of the armchairs. 'Now I'm up, I might as well stay up for a while.'

I was so glad she said that, because I couldn't stop shaking, and I needed her here with me, awake.

She rubbed at her backside. 'I'm getting bedsores with all this lying about. Have to get myself better. I'm never ill. Don't like being ill.' She said it as if she was angry at herself. As if her body was doing this deliberately to annoy her. I would have suggested the doctor again, but I saw that she was afraid. Afraid that something really was wrong with her.

I made her tea and toasted pancakes and we sat looking out at the view down the river. My hand trembled as I lifted the cup to my lips. I was scared.

'Your gran and I used to joke that we would sit out here in our wheelchairs when the time came.'

'I'm sorry it didn't work out like that, Aunt Belle.'

She waved that away. 'That's life, Tyler. You just have to accept it. When it's someone's time to die, it's their time.'

'Do you think that's true? I mean, that people have their time to die? Or do you think it might be possible to go back into the past and stop someone dying?'

She smiled. 'That's why you were on the laptop, wasn't it? You're working on a story?'

I smiled back and nodded, glad of the excuse to talk to

110

her about it. 'I'm thinking of a story about someone who can change the past. Go back in time and prevent someone's death. Do you think that's believable?'

'Well, Einstein said all time was happening simultaneously. And he was a genius. So, if that's true, then, yes, why can't you move in and out of other times. I like the idea of that story, Tyler. But I think you'd have to be careful. You should only save the people who are unlawfully dead.'

'Unlawfully dead?' I said.

'I think with some people it is their time to die, you know, if they die of natural causes. I don't think you should change that. But with the unlawfully dead – people who should not have died, because it wasn't their time, it was an accident, or murder, maybe even suicide – yes, I think you could change that. It would make a great story.'

The unlawfully dead. I liked the idea of that too.

Was Eleanor one of the unlawfully dead? Could I save her, so she could go on and expose Sister Kelly as the 'missing murderess'? I was sure that was what my gran wanted me to do. To make sure Sister Kelly's evil was exposed. Gran hadn't had time to find out the whole truth. But now I had the time and the opportunity. And a sudden realisation hit me. It wasn't Eleanor who had been keeping me here at all. It was Gran.

I had found out what my gran had already discovered. That Sister Kelly and Dorothy Blake and all of the others were one and the same. She had disappeared to this small town on the wild west coast of Scotland, but she hadn't stopped killing. The frail old Eleanor had been her next victim. Sister Kelly had still wanted to be seen as some kind of a saint. Looking after the old lady as if she was her own mother, yet, in reality, keeping her prisoner. A hero complex, they called it. She thrived on the excitement of seeming like a heroine, but she was no heroine, she was a villain.

And no one had ever guessed.

But now I knew.

Aunt Belle was shaking my arm. 'You were off in a dream there, Tyler. You know, if I did that they would say it was my age.'

She was ready to lie down again. I could see the weariness in her. I so wanted her to go back to being my lovely, funny, Aunt Belle. If only I could get her out of here. But she was afraid that if the doctor was called she would end up in hospital, and to tell the truth so was I.

Because where would I go if she went into hospital? I could not stay here on my own.

'I'll be on my feet tomorrow, you wait and see,' she said.

The house won't let you, I felt like saying. Sister Kelly won't allow it. I would have to do something to help her. And do it soon. I had to expose Sister Kelly, save Eleanor.

But what proof did I really have? An old photograph with a passing resemblance to a murderess. *I need more evidence, Gran,* I thought. *There has to be more.*

'You're off in a dream again, Tyler,' Aunt Belle said, as I helped her back into her room. You need a good night's sleep. So you have to promise me that you won't sleep in here tonight. Get into your own comfortable bed. If I need you, you're only a shout away.' Already her eyes were closing. 'Promise me, Tyler.'

But I could never sleep in that room, not with that shadow coming ever closer. I went back into the living room and watched the sun set. I'd never felt so alone. Not knowing what to do, or how to do it, if I did. And I was too tired to think about it. Aunt Belle was right. I needed a good night's sleep. But not in that room.

In the living room there was a big squashy sofa. I could sleep in here. No coldness in here. No shadows. And the sunset filled it with golden light. I took a soft velour throw from the chair in my aunt's room and checked on her once again. Then I went back into the living room, switched on the television and settled myself on the sofa.

I'd be able to sleep here. I shivered at the memory of that voice, that terrifying roar, but I pushed it to the back of my mind. A voice could not hurt me. I refused to be afraid. I was safe here, with the light on. With the television on. No evil in this room. Nothing could reach me here.

But I was wrong.

24

I dreamed. I was floating through the house, in the darkness, leaving the front room, winding my way along the hall and into Aunt Belle's room. I hovered over her as she lay sleeping, watching her draw laboured breaths before I moved away and floated once again into the hall. I came to the closed door of my own room, and I watched it slowly open, and though I knew I didn't want to – even in my dream I tried to pull myself away – I couldn't stop myself from moving forward. It was as if some unseen force was sucking me in. The room was in darkness. I could just make out the bed, the table beside it, the lamp. I tried to keep my eyes from that chair in the corner. But no matter how I tried, and oh, how I tried, my eyes were drawn there.

Don't look, Tyler. *Shut your eyes*, I prayed. But my eyes remained wide open. And fixed on that chair.

At first it seemed empty. I felt relief, but it only lasted for a moment. How long is a moment in a dream? Less than a heartbeat. Longer than a lifetime. And then something moved, something dark and shapeless. It seemed to rise from the chair. I shrank back. There was no form to it. No face. Yet I could feel its eyes on me. Eyes that petrified me. I wanted to get out of that room. But I couldn't move and the shape was rising from the chair, rising to my level, floating towards me, and I knew if I once saw its face, I would be finished. I began to shake. I tried to scream, but no sound came and the dark shadow was coming closer, closer, reaching out to me.

No!

I woke up, still shaking, but so relieved it was only a dream. I sat up. The room was lit by the flashing static of the television screen. I took a deep breath and tried to blot out that image, that shadow. Tried to wipe my memory clean of that nightmare.

I changed the channel. There had to be something on, something that would take my mind away from it. Anything would do. I finally found one of those American talk shows. Two young woman arguing about something, carefully orchestrated and meant to entertain. I started to watch it, but without wanting to, without meaning to, I fell asleep again.

Something was tugging at my cover. I pulled it back and turned on the sofa, tucking the throw round my chin. My feet were cold. Cold, as if fingers of ice were gripping my ankles.

My eyes opened. Another dream. Another nightmare.

Had to be.

Let it be.

But I was awake now. The room was in darkness. No television, no light, yet I hadn't switched either of them off. I lay still, too afraid to move. Something was there. Something moving. I was paralysed with fear.

I wanted it to be another dream. I would leap awake in a second. But no, this was real. I *was* awake, and something was next to the sofa. I could feel the icy cold of it near me. I couldn't breathe.

She was here. She'd found me. Nowhere was safe from her. Not for me.

I had to move. Had to get away. Yet, still I couldn't breathe.

My body was freezing into solid ice. Any closer and I'd be trapped.

I squeezed my eyes tight shut and leapt from the sofa, rolled across the floor. Didn't stop till I hit the wall on the other side of the room.

My shaking hand reached for the lamp and light flooded the room.

There was nothing there. The cover lay on the floor. The door of the front room was closed.

Another dream?

No.

She'd been here. I was getting too close to the truth about her, and she wanted to stop me.

Well, I was not going to let her.

I was going to get her first.

25

The final day

I sat the rest of that night in the safety of Gran's room just watching my aunt. I could not let her spend another night in this house. I had to get her out of here and tell the world about Sister Kelly. I had to make someone believe me. I had to make someone listen. Aunt Belle stirred in her sleep. She began to mutter. I crossed to her bed, but I couldn't make out what she was saying. Then her eyes opened. She smiled, but not at me. She was looking at some point behind me. I swung round, terrified. I was so afraid it was *her*, that she'd found her way into this room. But there was nothing there.

Aunt Belle closed her eyes and was soon asleep again. I felt her brow. It was cool to the touch, but beads of cold sweat pearled there. She was getting worse. I made a decision. I would call the doctor. I wanted her in a hospital. She would be safer there. At least till Steven came home. I would sleep on a chair by her bed in the hospital if I had to. But I had to get Aunt Belle out of here.

I started calling our surgery back home at eight o'clock, ringing every five minutes until finally my call was answered. The receptionist was full of sympathy, that is until I gave her our address. A coldness came into her voice then. 'The doctor couldn't come all the way down there. Why don't you call a local doctor?'

'I don't know any local doctors,' I said.

'Phone NHS Direct. They'll advise you,' she said. 'They're very helpful.'

I felt deflated when I came off the phone.

I was still standing in the hallway with the phone in my hand when the doorbell rang, shrill through the house.

It was the policeman who'd come to visit us before, Sergeant Ross. He stood there at the front door smiling, his big frame blocking the sun.

'Just thought I'd pop in to see how things are going. How's your arm?'

He was looking at the plaster I had there. I'd almost forgotten it. I waved his question away. 'It was nothing.' But I couldn't hide my relief at seeing him. 'I'm trying to get a doctor for my aunt.'

He stepped inside the door. 'A doctor? What's wrong with her?'

I wanted to tell him clearly and succinctly, without sounding like a drama queen. 'We both thought it was jet lag, but she's getting worse. She needs to see a doctor.' Once I started, it all came tumbling out. I couldn't stop myself. And, I was thinking, surely a policeman was the right person to tell? He would have to listen, wouldn't he?

'I have to get her out of this house. And I have information about the woman who used to live here, that Sister Kelly? She was a mass murderess.'

I told him all I'd found out about Sister Kelly. I even ran into the front room and brought back the book and the photograph. I could see he was listening carefully, taking it all in.

His expression didn't change. His face was like granite. 'And you found out all this in this book?' he asked.

I nodded my head. 'And on the internet. There's loads of stuff there too.' I wanted so much to convince him. Why couldn't I just keep my mouth shut? Because then I really blew it.

'And she's still here, haunting this house. She's the one making my aunt ill.'

121

His lips pursed, then his eyes creased in a smile. 'Ah, wait a minute, you're the lass that makes up the stories.'

'I'm not making this up. Sister Kelly is here!' I snapped at him, and his smile, what little there was of it, disappeared.

'I think you and your aunt *should* leave this house if you're having nightmares.'

'She needs to see a doctor,' I insisted.

'Ah well, there I can help you.' He took a notebook from his top pocket and began to write down a name. 'Local doctor. Doctor Gordon. Give him a buzz. Tell him Sergeant Ross gave you his name.'

He handed me the piece of paper. 'Will you pass on the information about Sister Kelly?'

He hesitated, looked out over the river. There was a windsurfer already there on the water. 'Based on an old photograph and stuff you read in a book? No. I will not,' he said at last. 'You should keep your stories for your notebooks.'

'This isn't a story. This is the truth.' But I knew then I couldn't convince him.

'You call the doctor for your auntie. I'll stop by tomorrow.' He turned and began to walk back to his car. I almost called out to him again. To force him to listen. But then I remembered.

I was the girl who was convinced I had seen my teacher, the teacher who had been dead for six months. I'd been laughed at, ridiculed, when I had tried to convince everyone at my last school about that. I had ended up being expelled. So how could I expect anyone to believe me now? I was just a girl, a girl with a history of telling stories.

It was obvious now that I had lost any trust Sergeant Ross might have had in me. No one was going to believe me about Sister Kelly.

Aunt Belle called out to me, her voice weak, 'Who was that?'

I went into her room, told her the sergeant had just been.

'Ooh, that big handsome sergeant?'

'Yeah. You'd better hurry up and get better, Aunt Belle. He might ask you for a date.'

And then she said something that floored me. Really scared me. 'I think it's too late for that, Tyler.'

I clutched at her hand. 'Too late for what?'

'If I tell you something, you won't be afraid, will you? Because I'm not.'

I was already afraid, but I said nothing.

'When our mother was dying, that would be your great-grandmother, Tyler,' Aunt Belle went on, 'she said she saw her mother standing in the corner, her father too. They'd come to lead her to heaven, that's what she kept saying.' Her voice weakened. I had to lean close to hear her. 'We thought she had dementia, didn't know what she was saying. But you know, later, after she died, your gran and I thought that maybe she *had* seen them. It was her time to die, and they knew it and they didn't want her to be afraid. They wanted to lead her on to the next world. And she wasn't afraid, Tyler.'

I held my breath, because I was sure I knew what was coming next. 'I think now is my time, Tyler.' Her eyes moved to the corner of the room, and she smiled at someone she saw standing there. I swung round again and there was nothing, but now I knew who it was she saw there. 'Your gran's come for me, Tyler, and I'm not afraid.'

26

I tried to tell myself she was raving. She had a fever; she was delirious. I felt like crying. I was completely alone. I couldn't handle all this by myself, but there was no one else, and now . . . I was certain my aunt was dying.

I would not cry. There was no time to feel sorry for myself. I lifted the phone and punched in the number Sergeant Ross had given me. It was busy.

I went into the kitchen and poured myself a glass of orange juice and opened the patio doors. I looked along the beach at the surf roaring in. There were people walking along the shore, the warm wind blowing through their hair, filling their clothes. There was a family setting up for a day at the seaside, laying a tartan blanket on the rocks, unpacking their car as their children ran and laughed and played in the water. Free.

And I was trapped here. I couldn't leave Aunt Belle now, not for a moment.

I tried to call Paul Forbes. I needed to talk to someone. His phone didn't even ring. *NUMBER NOT IN USE*, came up on the screen. Not in use? And he had told me to call him anytime, day or night? I would have laughed if I hadn't been so close to tears. I tried again, just in case it was a mistake, but again got the same message. *NUMBER NOT IN USE*.

And there in the kitchen I did cry, couldn't stop myself.

I didn't want to stay here for another night. The thought terrified me. If I could get Aunt Belle into the hospital, I could stay the night there with her. I'd sleep on the floor, in the foyer, anywhere. I'd refuse to leave.

Gran had kept me here for a purpose, to find out about Sister Kelly. I had done that. At that moment all I knew was that I could not stay another night in this house.

It was Aunt Belle calling out to me that brought me back. 'I'm coming,' I called and I splashed my face with water and pulled myself together.

She needed help to get to the toilet and as I took her arm I felt how weak she'd become. In just a few days, my robust, funny aunt was weak and shaky.

Don't die on me, Aunt Belle, I prayed. *Not you too.*

After I got her back into bed, I tried the doctor again. The number was still busy. Then I went into the bedroom and sat with Aunt Belle and watched the gulls flying over the water.

I even tried calling Steven, but his mobile was switched off.

At midday, I tried the doctor again, and this time my call was answered.

I was so excited I babbled the whole thing out. But as soon as I mentioned that we were here on holiday and Doctor Gordon wasn't my doctor, I heard the ice form in the receptionist's voice.

'Doctor Gordon is very busy . . .'

'Oh, please, my aunt's not well, and we're all alone here. I don't know what to do.'

She softened. 'If you call back after three, you can talk to the doctor personally. OK?'

'You promise you won't forget?'

Wrong thing to say. She froze again. 'If I say I'll tell the doctor, I'll tell the doctor.'

She'd rung off before I could apologise. I checked my watch. 1.20. Not too long to wait, and then, I'd ask the doctor to come. I'd make him come. I'd tell him I thought she was dying. And once I was out of this house, I would make someone listen. I would expose Sister Kelly, whatever it took.

I went back into the kitchen to make myself a sandwich for lunch. I got some bread, some cheese from the fridge, and I pulled open the drawer and lifted out a knife when something caught my eye. Crawling along the worktop was a spider. A huge spider. I gazed at it, mesmerised . . .

And the drawer slammed shut on my fingers.

The pain was so agonising I couldn't even yell. I stepped back, felt myself go faint, and then the kitchen door closed.

My fingers blazed with pain. I knew I had to get out of here. I stumbled to the door and tried to pull it open. It wouldn't budge. As if someone on the other side was holding it shut.

The doors to the garden still lay open. I could get out that way. I flew towards them, but I wasn't quick enough. They slammed shut too.

Clouds covered the sun. The room grew dark.

She was here.

'Leave us be!' I yelled it out, trying desperately to pull at the kitchen door. I was locked in.

The shelf on the wall above me trembled. I stepped back but I wasn't fast enough. The shelf broke loose, pots and pans, everything, came crashing down on top of me. I tried to protect myself, folding my arms above my head. I let out a yell of pain as a cast-iron oven dish landed on my bruised fingers and I slipped on the tiled floor.

My head cracked against the wall. Above me on the edge of the worktop I saw the sharp blade of the knife. I held up my arm again.

'No!' I yelled.

27

I lifted my arm and saw blood trickling down. I was lying on the floor, must have fainted.

There was a movement in the hall. Something outside the door. I closed my eyes. I couldn't bear to look.

The door opened. I heard soft footsteps. The first thing I saw when I opened my eyes was Paul Forbes crouching over me, looking concerned.

I sat up. The kitchen was tidy again. Where was the broken shelf? The tumbled pots and pans? There was no chaos in the kitchen. The patio doors lay open, the curtains fluttered at the open window, the fresh smell of the sea blowing in. I tried to stand up.

'The shelf fell down,' I said.

Paul followed my gaze. The shelf was steady, piled with pots and pans and dishes.

'The knife . . .' I muttered. The knife was on the floor.

'That's a nasty cut.'

My arm *was* bleeding. At least that was some proof. 'I didn't do this. *She* did it. She locked me in here.'

But I could see in his eyes he doubted me. Even Paul, who had experienced so much in this house, doubted what I was saying.

'It happened. You know it happened. You know what she can do.'

I remembered then he knew nothing of what I had found out. Nothing of how evil Sister Kelly really was. As he helped me to my feet, I tried to tell him everything I had discovered.

Paul wrapped a kitchen towel round my arm. 'I think you might need stitches,' he said.

I clutched at him. 'You have to believe me, Paul. I've found out who she really is, and she doesn't want me to tell anyone. She's trying to stop me.' I dragged him into the living room. 'I'll show you. Read this book.' I pushed the book into his hands. 'Chapter ten. Read Chapter ten. "The Missing Murderess".'

He skimmed through the pages as I watched the blood seep through the paper towel. He was looking at the photograph.

'You think all these women are Sister Kelly?'

'That's exactly what I think.'

I slumped into a chair. I felt weak. 'I think my gran had found out about her too . . . but she died before she could do anything about it.'

'And what can we do?'

We – how I loved the sound of that word. I wasn't alone.

'Find some kind of real proof. I don't know. I just know we have to tell somebody.'

Paul looked at my arm. 'You really are going to need that stitched.'

And that's when I remembered the doctor. I checked the time. 2.55. How long had I been in that kitchen?

No matter. It was almost three. Surely, I could call him now.

It was the same officious receptionist who answered. 'I phoned earlier,' I reminded her, 'about my aunt? You said I should call at three?'

'Oh yes, I remember,' she said. 'I'm sorry, but the doctor's been called out on an emergency.'

'But my aunt isn't well, and now I've cut my arm, and you said he'd be there!'

I didn't mean to shout. Didn't even realise I was shouting. I heard her draw in her breath.

'The doctor's been called out on a *real* emergency,' she said it as if mine wasn't. 'I mean, what are you calling for exactly? Your aunt or your cut arm?'

I could feel the anger building in me. 'Can't you get the doctor on his mobile? Tell him to call here too?'

'You're not even one of his patients,' she snapped back. 'If your arm's that bad, get yourself to a hospital.' Then she rang off.

'I don't think that's bad advice,' Paul said when I told him. 'Your arm needs attention.'

I shook my head. 'I can't leave my aunt.' Then a thought struck me. What was Paul doing here?

'I've been trying to call you,' he said when I asked him. 'It kept coming up number not in use. I thought something must be wrong.'

'I tried calling you too, and it was the same thing, number not in use!'

Paul shrugged. 'Signal's rubbish down here.'

But I doubted that was the reason. This was Sister Kelly's work again.

'Look, now I'm here I can help. You go to the hospital, and I'll stay with your aunt.'

'You'd stay here, after everything that happened to you?' I couldn't believe he was offering to do this.

'I'll sit with your aunt, in her room. It's broad daylight. And you'll be back long before dark. I'm not scared during the day.'

'But look what she did just now in the kitchen.'

He hesitated, and I could see he wasn't quite prepared to believe that anything had attacked me in there. He probably thought that my own fear, my overactive imagination had made me fall with the knife in my hand. I wished I could believe that myself.

'I . . . I can't leave you here. What if my aunt wakes up and there's a strange boy in her room?'

'Do you think she will wake up?' Paul said, and I knew she wouldn't.

He was already on the phone. 'I'm calling for a taxi to take you to Accident and Emergency. The sooner you go, the sooner you'll come back. We'll talk then. There has to be something we can do.'

'But Aunt Belle.'

'I'll keep phoning for the doctor. I promise.'

As I waited for the taxi, I asked him over and over again if he would be OK in the house.

'I'm not going to move out of that room, Tyler.'

But Sister Kelly was growing stronger, more powerful. Who knew what she could do?

'You have to promise me you'll be careful, Paul.'

He stood at the door as the taxi drove off. I watched him from the back window waving and smiling. It was such a good feeling to know I wasn't alone in this any more.

28

I had expected a long wait at the hospital, but Accident and Emergency wasn't too busy and the receptionist told me I'd be seen within half an hour.

A nurse took me into a cubicle not long after I arrived and checked that the bleeding had stopped. She wrapped a temporary dressing around it, then sent me back to wait to see a doctor.

I took out my phone and punched in our house's land-line number. Paul answered on the third ring. 'I'm fine,' he said at once. 'OK? I've even left the room to go to the toilet, didn't like to use your aunt's en suite. Nothing happened.'

I saw the receptionist approaching me. My turn, I thought, standing up.

She pointed to a sign on the wall.

MOBILE PHONES MUST BE SWITCHED OFF.

'I'm afraid you can't use that here,' she said.

'Sorry,' I said, and into the phone I said to Paul, 'I'll call you later.' And I added softly, 'And please, be careful.'

I closed the phone over and apologised again. Then I sat watching the clock, praying for the minute hand to move more quickly and all the while I sat there my imagination went haywire.

I had left my aunt with a complete stranger. She might wake up and see him sitting there beside her bed and, well, what would she do? Scream? Faint? Not Aunt Belle. She would most likely attack Paul. The thought made me smile, but only for a second, because what if Paul wasn't what he seemed, even now was rifling through Aunt Belle's bags and purses, looking for money, jewellery.

And all the time the clock ticked on ever so slowly.

I stood up and went out through the automatic doors and phoned again.

'Is that you on your way home?' Paul asked, and when I hesitated he added, 'Or are you just checking up on me?'

'I'm sorry.' All I seemed to be doing was apologise.

'Stop worrying, Tyler. The sun is shining, your aunt is sleeping and I'm reading that book. Wow! If you're right and Sister Kelly really is all these other women, what a story! But how can we prove it?'

We again, it made my spirits soar. 'You should check out the stuff I found out about her on my laptop.'

I went back inside feeling better and took my seat once more, and waited. It seemed everyone was watching me. The receptionist behind the glass in her booth kept glancing at me suspiciously, waiting for me to whip out my phone again. Orderlies passed pushing trolleys, their eyes seeking me out. I was sure of it. And time ticked on slowly.

The hands of the clock clicked exactly on the half-hour when a nurse appeared at the door of the waiting room. 'Tyler Lawless?' she called out.

I stood up and followed her along a corridor and into a curtained booth. 'Doctor will be with you shortly.'

'You mean I've got to wait again?'

Her smile wavered. 'The doctor will be with you as quickly as possible.'

I phoned Paul again. It rang and rang, and I imagined the house still and silent except for that ringing phone, saw my aunt still sleeping, and the phone lying on the floor and Paul . . . nowhere. An open door, an empty room.

I jumped in surprise when he answered. 'Tyler, give me a break.'

'I'm sorry, I don't know why I'm so worried, it's as if I know something is going to happen.'

'Well, I can't feel anything. Honest. Your aunt hasn't stirred.'

The curtain was suddenly pulled across and the doctor stepped in. *Doctor Ho*, his badge read. 'You are not allowed to use your phone in here.'

Another muttered apology and I switched the phone off without even a goodbye.

The nurse appeared behind the doctor. Her face was grim. 'She's been warned about that before,' she said it as if I was some kind of persistent troublemaker.

Doctor Ho unwrapped the dressing from my arm. The gash looked to me like a gaping mouth. My legs turned to jelly.

'How did this happen?' he asked.

I wished I could tell him the truth. I looked into his eyes. I wasn't good at lies.

His eyes moved to mine. My hesitation wasn't impressing him at all. 'How did this happen?' he asked again.

'I was making a sandwich . . . and the knife slipped.'

His long fingers moving around my arm, stopped. Again his eyes met mine. 'It must have slipped with a lot of force to give you a cut like this.'

'What do you mean?' My voice was shaking.

Did I look guilty? I must have. The nurse whispered something to the doctor behind her closed hand.

'Have you ever cut yourself like this before?' he asked now.

And my eyes automatically shot to the cut on my other arm. He saw it too. It was obviously what the nurse had spotted. 'That,' I stuttered, 'that was an accident too.'

But what they were thinking hit me like a brick. Self-harm.

'You think I did this to *myself*!' I shouted, though I didn't mean to. 'It was an accident!'

Yet, even as I said it, I knew I sounded as if I was telling a lie. But I *was* lying. Because it wasn't an accident. Sister Kelly had been responsible for that too. And I couldn't tell them that.

The doctor took a deep breath. 'You're going to need a few stitches,' he said and then turned to the nurse. 'Get it cleaned up and stitched.'

The nurse began cleaning up my wound. 'Will this take long? I have to get back home.' I tried to explain as calmly as I could. 'Look, my aunt's not well. I've been trying to get a doctor for her. I'm on my own, I need to get back to her.'

And all the while I spoke I knew I was giving them more reasons that would make them think I would self-harm. I had too many problems for a teenager to cope with.

'Would you like to speak to a social worker? They might be able to help.'

That was the last thing I needed. I just wanted to get out of this hospital and to be back with Aunt Belle.

'No, no. I'm sorry,' I said. 'I'll be fine.'

Twenty minutes later I was stitched and bandaged and ready to leave. In the foyer I opened my phone to call a taxi, but the receptionist rapped at the glass of her booth and shook her head. She pointed outside.

I looked back as I stepped through the automatic doors. Doctor Ho was deep in conversation with a policeman. And of course the policeman, probably the only policeman in this little community, had to be Sergeant Ross. They were talking about me, no doubt about that. As I looked, they both turned to me. Sergeant Ross nodded, acknowledging something Doctor Ho was saying. That I was a danger to myself probably. To make matters worse, I began to run as if I was guilty. As if they might just come after me.

The whole time I waited at the taxi rank I expected one of them to come racing out of the doors. I was desperate to get away. As soon as I was in the taxi, I phoned Paul again to let him know I was on my way, I'd be back soon.

The phone rang and rang and finally went on to the answering machine. 'Paul, call me as soon as you get this.'

I tried his mobile after that. Once again there was no answer, only that same message. *NUMBER NOT IN USE.* I sent a text just in case he could access it. I called the house again. And still there was no answer.

All the way along the sun-scorched coast road, I phoned. And he didn't answer.

Something was wrong.

29

When the taxi pulled up, the house looked quiet, as if all was well. Paul hadn't heard the phone, I kept telling myself. That was all.

The driver turned to me. 'Home safe and sound, hen,' he said.

A part of me wanted to ask him to come into the house with me, but it would sound so silly.

'Are you feeling OK?' he asked. And before I could reply he went on. 'Somebody should have gone to that hospital with you. A young lassie like you, and you got stitches. You shouldn't have had to go on your own.'

'I'm fine, really,' I said.

And for all his concern, he was gone, almost as soon as I stepped from the back seat.

I took a deep breath and opened the door. I knew right away that something *was definitely* wrong. The house was silent. I called out, 'Paul?' but there was no answer. I walked past the open door of the living room, then looked into the dining room. Empty, both of them. I walked to Aunt Belle's room and pushed open the door. Paul wasn't there. Aunt Belle lay quiet, breathing heavily. She didn't sound well at all. The book lay on the floor, spine open, as if Paul had been reading it when something had disturbed him he had let it drop from his fingers.

'Paul!' I called his name again and Aunt Belle stirred, then lay still. Nothing was going to wake her up for now.

I stood in the hall and stared at the closed door of the other bedroom. I stood staring at it, willing it to open, not wanting to have to go in there, knowing I had no choice.

Then, it appeared. A spider the size of my hand crawling up the door. I knew what that meant. She was close. She was here.

It was now or never. I took a deep breath and I ran at that door, had to or my courage would have failed me. I flung the door wide open and there he was. Paul, lying on his back on the floor, his eyes wide open, staring in terror.

Though I couldn't see her, I knew she was here.

'You're not getting him,' I yelled, and I gripped Paul's ankles and began to drag him out of that room. 'You're not getting him!' I repeated it, but even then I was afraid I was too late. Paul looked dead!

He was heavier than I imagined – a dead weight. I didn't want to think like that. Dead. Yet, even as I dragged him, I could see the door begin to close. She was trying to keep us in here. There was no way I was going to allow that. I shoved that door wide open again. 'No!' I yelled. And with one more pull I had Paul in the hallway and the door slammed shut.

I leaned over him. 'Paul?' I looked into his eyes, but there was no recognition there. Whatever terror they were seeing was blocking everything else from his view.

Why had he gone into that room? And in the same instant I thought it, I remembered what I'd said about there being more information on my laptop. My laptop was on the bed in that room. Had he thought he would be safe to step in, just for a moment, get the laptop and go back into the safety of my aunt's room? I could understand why he thought he'd be safe. It had been broad daylight. But Sister Kelly had been too quick for him. As soon as he was inside, the door had slammed shut behind him, the room darkened, and she had come out of the shadows.

He was still breathing at least, his chest rising and falling steadily, but no matter how I tried to shake him back into consciousness his eyelids didn't flicker.

My finger trembled as I punched in 999, and told them I needed an ambulance fast. Then I slumped to the floor beside Paul, as if I could protect him from anything that might come at him through that door.

The ambulance arrived and I had no explanation for what had happened to Paul. All I said was that I'd left him with my aunt and came back to find him like this. A police car pulled up behind the ambulance and Sergeant Ross stepped from it.

'I thought that 999 call was from this address,' he said. He explained to the paramedics, as if I wasn't there, that I had been at the hospital earlier. 'An unexplained accident.' I could almost see the inverted commas.

And now, another unexplained accident. The paramedics looked at me, looked at my arm.

I couldn't stop myself from babbling out. 'It was Sister Kelly. She haunts this house. She did it all.' I regretted it as soon as I spoke. Now they would think I was crazy.

Sergeant Ross let out a long sigh. 'You're saying a ghost did all this?'

The paramedics shared a knowing smile. 'You should hear some of the things teenagers tell us. Ghosts, vampires, zombies. You name it, we've heard it.'

Sergeant Ross looked into my aunt's room. 'Your aunt doesn't look so good, does she?'

'I've been trying to get a doctor all day.'

And then a terrible thought came to me. Did Sergeant Ross think all of this was my doing? If they thought at the hospital I had been self-harming because I wanted attention, it wasn't a giant leap to believe that to get more attention I had done something to Paul, to my aunt.

'What's wrong with him?' I asked as they were getting ready to carry Paul out to the ambulance.

'We'll have a better idea when we get him to the hospital,' one of them told me.

'Do you know where the boy lives?' Sergeant Ross asked me. 'We'll have to inform his parents.'

I gave him the address. 'He has a mobile. His home number might be there,' I added.

Sergeant Ross fumbled in Paul's pocket and took out

the phone. He looked at me. 'I'm also calling a doctor to have a look at your aunt.'

And for a second my heart lifted. At last, a doctor was coming to see Aunt Belle.

30

'So, the truth now. What exactly happened here?' Sergeant Ross and I sat in the front room as we waited for the doctor. 'And please, no more of this, "It was Sister Kelly's ghost who did it."'

What was the point of telling the truth? 'I had an accident with the knife,' I sighed. 'I was making a sandwich. Paul arrived just when it happened and he insisted I go to the hospital. He said he'd stay here with my aunt and when I came back he was like . . . how you saw him.'

There, I thought, did he prefer that version? Was that more acceptable?

'You found him lying in the hall?'

'He was in the other bedroom.'

'So, why didn't you just leave him there. Why drag him into the hall?'

Well, I wasn't going to lie about that. I looked straight at him. 'I don't like that room.'

His face creased into a smile. 'That will be the haunted room then?' He stood up. 'Mind if I go in? I've always wanted to see a ghost.'

'You can laugh, but you'll see, the door won't stay open . . . and it's ice cold in there.'

He pushed open the door and I stood back as he stepped inside.

I waited for the door to swing shut. Then he'd see. He'd know I was telling the truth.

The door stayed open.

'Doesn't feel cold to me at all,' he said. He turned to me.

'She's sly,' I murmured.

'A sly ghost?'

He came back into the hall. 'So you dragged him out here.'

'Paul's parents will tell you there's something in this house. Paul's mother saw something in that room too.'

'Oh, I will be talking to them,' he said, as if it was a warning.

After that, we sat in stony silence until the doctor arrived.

Doctor Gordon looked every inch the country doctor, from an old-fashioned tweed suit, to the doctor's bag he carried.

'Right, let's see what we have here,' he said as I led him into Aunt Belle's room.

I began to babble again. 'At first she thought it was just jet lag, and then we thought maybe she'd caught a bug.'

At that point Sergeant Ross bent and whispered something in Doctor Gordon's ear. No doubt something about me. Then the doctor asked me to leave so he could have a proper look at my aunt.

A few minutes later, he came out of the room. 'What have you been giving her?'

'Just a vitamin drink I got from Mrs De Luca at the village shop.'

'Could you show it to me, please?' he said.

I took him into the kitchen and lifted the bottle from the shelf. He sniffed at it. 'Did you put anything else in it when you gave it to her?'

I looked from him to Sergeant Ross. I couldn't believe what I was hearing. 'Are you honestly suggesting I put something in my aunt's vitamin drink?'

The doctor shrugged. 'I only asked a question.'

Had something been added to that vitamin drink? If it had, I knew who would have done that.

'Maybe your ghost added something, eh?' Sergeant Ross said as if he could read my mind.

I turned on him. 'You can't believe I did anything to my aunt!'

Yet even as I said it I was remembering Mrs De Luca's comment about my obsession with people dying. Remembering the estate agent's startled look when Aunt Belle joked that I was trying to poison her because I was her sole heir. The police would find all that out. Guilt was closing around me.

'I'm admitting your aunt to hospital,' Doctor Gordon said.

I slumped against the wall with relief. At last she would be getting out of this house.

'Can I go to the hospital with her?'

'Of course,' the sergeant said. And it was quite clear to me that he wasn't planning to let me out of his sight.

While we waited for the ambulance, I gathered up clothes and toiletries for my aunt, hoping they would notice how caring I was. But when I glanced at them, the doctor was handing the bottle with my aunt's vitamin drink to the sergeant, and he slipped it into a bag. I felt suddenly faint. I was in so much trouble, and I'd done nothing wrong.

The doctor came back into the bedroom and lifted the photo of Gran and Aunt Belle on the bedside table. 'Is this your grandmother?' he asked.

I stood beside him. Gran looked so happy, smiling, arm in arm with her sister. 'Yes. Her and my aunt Belle are sisters. Did you know her?'

'Not exactly know. Mrs Crawford, wasn't it? I was the one who put her in hospital when she had the heart attack. She was a nice lady.'

How I wished she was here now to help me.

I almost missed what he said next I was thinking of her so hard. 'I really think it was that fall that brought on her heart attack.'

I stopped, my hands halfway to Aunt Belle's bag. 'What did you say? What fall?'

'I think it was the day before she died, she fell down the cellar steps. When I finally saw her, all she could say, over and over, was "the cellar". It wasn't a bad fall. She was only bruised. But she seemed quite shaken and I think if she hadn't had that fall, she probably wouldn't have had the heart attack.'

31

There was no time to think about what Doctor Gordon had said. Too much was happening too quickly. Right at that moment the ambulance came for Aunt Belle. I was allowed – although I was sure by the look that passed between Doctor Gordon and Sergeant Ross, allowed reluctantly – to travel in the ambulance with my aunt. Sergeant Ross would probably have preferred me to travel in the police car. The paramedic kept his eye on me as I sat clutching Aunt Belle's hand.

She'll be all right now, I said to myself. She was out of that house, she'd be all right now.

Worse was to come when we reached the hospital. Paul's mother was waiting there at the entrance. As soon as she saw me she flew at me, such a rage within her. '*You* did this to my boy! *You!*'

One of the medics tried to hold her back. She pushed him aside. 'Did she tell you she came to my house? She lured my son to that house of hers. Now he's in a coma. He might not live, and if he dies . . .' Again, she sprang at me.

Though I was afraid, here at least was my witness. Here was someone who could tell them there was something in the house. Something evil.

Sergeant Ross had just arrived. I grabbed his arm. 'She'll tell you.' I pleaded with him to listen. 'They were renting our house, and they just packed up one day and left. Something terrified her. She can tell you. The house is haunted.' I turned my eyes to her. 'You know it is. Tell him!'

She stared at me. Silenced.

'Is this true Mrs Forbes?' Sergeant Ross asked her.

She hesitated for only a moment. 'Of course it's not true. Haven't you heard about her lies?' She looked back to me, venom filled her eyes. 'I found out about you, Tyler Lawless.' She spat out my name as if she was swearing. 'You claimed you saw the ghost of your teacher when you were in your last school. Caused nothing but trouble – and now, you're at it again.'

I would never be allowed to forget that. Never.

A nurse ran up to us then. 'Do you realise you're in a hospital? I can't have you screaming like this.'

Mrs Forbes' eyes never left me. 'Blame her!' Her finger jabbed against me. 'She's the only something evil in that house.'

I had no one here who knew me, who could vouch for me. No one who knew the kind of person I was. I was in a strange town, with no family around me, or friends. Now, I didn't even have Aunt Belle.

Mrs Forbes was led off, crying. I would have felt sorry for her if I hadn't seen so much hate in her eyes. A police-woman came over.

'This is PC Glinn,' Sergeant Ross said. 'She'll stay with you.'

I felt as if I was in custody already.

PC Glinn smiled. 'Call me Valerie,' she said, and she sat with me while Aunt Belle was examined and finally moved to a room in one of the wards. I couldn't think of anything except her and Paul. Was she going to be all right? Was Paul?

'We'll get in touch with your parents,' Valerie said, breaking into my thoughts.

'I don't want you to do that.'

She shrugged. 'I'm afraid we have no choice.'

As I walked into the room where Aunt Belle lay, I knew she was no longer asleep. She was burning up now, in a high fever. Unconscious.

I wasn't left alone with her. Valerie sat in the room with me. Me on one side of the bed, her on the other. When I reached to take Aunt Belle's hand in mine, I saw her tense. And when Aunt Belle stirred and I lifted a glass of water to wet her lips, Valerie reached across and took it from me. 'I'll see to that,' she said.

I curled up in a chair in the corner and tried not to cry. They thought I might harm her, even here. And tomorrow they were going to phone Mum and Dad. I couldn't hold back the tears then, and I sobbed. Valerie looked over at me, offered me a tissue, but little sympathy. She'd probably seen too much evil masquerading behind tears.

I had changed the past once – why couldn't I do it this time?

Because I didn't know how! And I didn't know what thing in the past to change? I'd thought at first I'd been meant to save Eleanor. Hadn't she asked me to help her? I was meant to save her so she could go on to expose Sister Kelly. But how was I supposed to do that?

What was the good of having a power if you didn't know how to use it?

And what if I wasn't meant to save Eleanor at all?

Maybe I was meant to help Paul?

Or my aunt Belle?

How was I ever going to bring Sister Kelly to justice? Who was going to believe a stroppy teenager with a history of telling tall tales?

I was useless. Useless.

The person I really wanted to save was my gran. Aunt Belle had said I shouldn't change the past of those who had died natural deaths. Like Gran. How could I stop her having a heart attack?

Impossible.

I sat up in the chair. Looked across at Valerie. She was busy reading her magazine.

Impossible . . . unless . . .

My mind was racing. The doctor's words came back to me.

If she hadn't had that fall, she probably wouldn't have had the heart attack.

She fell in the cellar.

Why did she go down there? One answer came to me. Sister Kelly.

And what made her fall? Again only one answer. Sister Kelly.

Gran *was* one of the 'unlawfully dead'.

And in that instant I knew what I had to do – and how to do it.

If I could stop my gran from falling in the cellar, she wouldn't have the heart attack. She'd still be alive. Her house wouldn't have been rented out. I'd never have met the Forbes. Paul wouldn't be in a coma and Aunt Belle wouldn't be in this hospital.

I could change everything, and then Gran and I could expose the truth about who Sister Kelly really was.

I would have my gran back.

My gran, alive again. The thought of it made my heart leap.

All I had to do was get out of this hospital. And go down into that cellar again.

32

I got to my feet and Valerie looked up from her magazine. 'Can I go to the toilet?' I asked.

She couldn't stop me, I knew that. After all, I wasn't under arrest and she was only there to watch me when I was with Aunt Belle. After a moment, she nodded. 'Yes, of course.'

To my horror she stood up as if she was ready to come with me. 'I can go on my own!' Did I say it too quickly? Luckily she took it as genuine teenage embarrassment.

'Don't worry, I'm not going with you.'

What she did was almost as bad. She stood at the door of Aunt Belle's room and watched me as I walked to the female toilet at the end of the corridor. I was convinced she planned to stay there till I came out. But I had to get out of this hospital.

There wasn't even a window I could open in the

toilet, even if I did have the nerve to leap from the second floor to the ground. I stood for a moment, thinking. I looked around. What there was, hanging on a hook on the wall, was a blue hospital gown, and a Zimmer frame in the corner. A disguise. But could I carry it off?

I had no choice. The gown almost came to my ankles, and I pulled my hair back and bent my shoulders like a sick patient. I took a deep breath and, pushing the Zimmer in front of me, I hobbled out of the toilet.

I didn't glance back. I imagined Valerie standing there, seeing the blue-gowned patient edging her way down the corridor.

My breath came in short gasps. I was waiting for her to shout after me, call my name. I expected at any second to hear her footsteps running behind me. I kept shuffling forward, trying not to rush. Sick people can't rush. Step by step I was getting closer to the door.

And still she didn't come.

I turned the corner at last. Out of her sight, I shoved the Zimmer aside, pulled off the gown and began to run. I took the stairs, and on the ground floor, made sure no one was about before I began walking to the automatic doors. I didn't start running again until I was outside, heading for the taxi rank. To my relief, one taxi was there. I was in the back seat in a second.

'You sound as if you should be in the hospital, not leaving it,' the taxi driver said when he heard my heavy breathing.

I told him where I wanted to go and then I sat back and watched the night settle over the shore.

I had to get to the house before Valerie realised I wouldn't be coming back and raised the alarm. I pictured her checking her watch, beginning to wonder what was keeping me. Going down to the toilet, pushing open the door, calling my name.

And then what?

I mean, I wasn't a hardened criminal – there wouldn't be a full-scale alert out for me. Perhaps just a call on her mobile to alert Sergeant Ross.

Yet when I heard a police siren coming behind us, I stiffened. Afraid it was me they were after.

The taxi driver pulled into the side of the road to let them pass. He laughed. 'Late for their tea break probably.'

I tried to laugh too, but it sounded more like hysteria.

'Visiting somebody at the hospital then?' he asked me. 'My aunt,' I said. 'But she's going to be fine. Now,' I added softly. And when I changed the past . . . she would never have been sick at all.

I was afraid. More afraid than I'd ever been in my life. But I was excited too.

Me. Tyler Lawless. I could change the past.

And bring back my gran.

That thought alone made any danger, any terror worthwhile.

We turned off the road and up the track to the house. It lay in darkness. Waiting. Waiting for me. The moon glinted silver on the river.

'Beautiful setting,' the driver said as I paid him. 'It must be a pleasure living here.'

'It will be,' I said, and I could see his puzzled frown.

I took a deep breath as I put the key in the door. I opened it wide and stepped inside.

The house was silent. I stood for a moment listening. Then I shouted.

'I'm back, Sister Kelly!'

33

I stood in the dark hallway with the moonlight streaming in through the window above the front door. The
stained glass turned the silver light into a myriad of
colours that played across the walls. I walked from room
to room. What was I looking for? For a moment my
courage failed me. I wanted to run back to the hospital,
face any repercussions there might be. Almost at the
same time a voice spoke silently in my mind, and it was
my gran's.

'Help me, Tyler.'

There could be no other answer. 'I will.' I said it aloud,
pushing every doubt I had from my mind.

I stood in her room, felt her comforting presence
giving me the strength I needed to make me go on. She
would show me. She would help me. I could almost hear
her speak. 'You have to do this, Tyler. Be brave.'

I stepped back into the hall and my heart leapt with fear.

The hatch to the cellar was open.

The chest of drawers was once more back against the wall. I stepped towards the opening.

The cold air of a tomb gusted up towards me. I looked down. The stairs disappeared into blackness. My hand was shaking as I took a step down. I reached for the switch and flooded the cellar with light. Was I really going down there? How could I be so sure my gran would protect me?

And yet in that same instant close behind me, I heard her words again, so close, so real. 'Help me, Tyler.'

The words made my heart almost burst. She was here, urging me on. Only I could save her from that fall.

I took another step down. The cellar was bright, and empty. No shadows here. Yet with each step I expected to see that dark shadow, the shadow that had sat in the corner of my room, and the spiders that heralded her presence.

But there was nothing here. Just an empty white space, and again doubt rose in me. I reached the bottom. There was nothing here. I turned in a circle, looking from bare wall to bare wall. No shadows, no menacing presence, nothing.

And then, something changed. The floor seemed to sway under my feet. The light went out and the cellar was plunged into darkness. And someone stepped down from the hall above.

I looked up.

Can your heart really break? Break into tiny pieces like a crushed eggshell? Because I was sure mine did at that moment.

I was looking at my gran.

Alive. Warm. She was wearing the green sweater I had given her one Christmas. I wanted to call out to her, but my voice was frozen in my throat. I couldn't move, though I so wanted to reach out and touch her.

She couldn't see me. Once again, I was like a ghost from the future, watching. She took another step down, swinging her torch around, its light cutting into the dark. She swung the beam from here to there, searching for something.

There was a sound. I heard it, and so did she. We both gasped and listened. Whispered words. Pleading, 'Help me. Help me.' It was Eleanor's voice. I was sure of it.

'How can I can help you?' We both asked it at the same time. Gran in her time. Me in mine. 'How?'

Something stirred in the cellar. The walls seemed to come alive. They seemed to shimmer and move and something began to emerge from behind those walls. A shape not quite substance, shade and shadow.

A figure like smoke. It became form. An old woman stepped out from behind the walls. It was Eleanor.

My gran let out a cry. 'Oh my God, she kept you down here.' There was a sob of pure horror in her voice.

And in that second the truth of it hit me. This was what Gran had discovered and hadn't been able to tell anyone. She had discovered Eleanor walled up down here. Proof at last of Sister Kelly's evil.

And then I heard Eleanor's whispered voice. 'I knew you would help me, Tyler. I knew.'

And that was the moment my gran realised I was there with her. Her time and mine fusing into one.

'Tyler?'

'Gran?' I called her name and she turned, and I knew she saw me. Perhaps a wraith, perhaps like smoke, but I knew she saw me. 'Gran!!!' I shouted it, but my voice was like some distant echo.

Her eyes filled with tears. 'Oh, Tyler . . .' Her hand reached out to me.

Then there was another sound like the rumble of thunder, an ominous sound, and in the same instant Eleanor's ghostly figure began to shuffle, terrified, back into her walled tomb. In death, just as scared as she had been in life. She held out her hand to me, her face barely discernible. 'Help me, Tyler.' Not even a whisper of a voice. Wanting her body found, wanting Sister Kelly brought to justice.

The thunder became a roar and the shadow of evil filled the cellar. It was heading for Gran. This was the moment when she would fall, stumbling, tumbling down those steps. That shadow loomed over her and I knew I had to stop it. This was the moment I could change everything!

'Gran! Run! Get away now!'

And she heard me. I knew she heard me, though the sight of me was lost to her now. 'Tyler?'

I saw the shadow speed towards her – it would be upon her any second, and I couldn't let that happen. Gran had to get out of this cellar, tell her story. She had to.

I yelled again, 'Run!' and I threw myself between her and the dark terrifying shape that was there.

Gran hesitated for only the split of a second, then she was up those stairs. I called after her. 'Tell them, Gran. Tell them everything.'

Did she hear me? I don't know, but she ran up those steps and out of the cellar. She didn't fall. I had stopped that.

The roar grew, and the shadow turned and came for me. I would not look at the face. Sure looking at that face would bring more terror than I could handle. I flung my arms across my eyes and felt ice envelop me, dragging me down. I struggled against it. 'No!'

I was caught in a whirlwind, sure I was about to fly away. My ears stung. My heart raced. I turned and I twisted. I had no power over my body.

And then, I was the one who fell.

34

The cellar swirled around me. My eyes stayed tight shut until I was sure everything was still again. Only then did I open them. I was in the same cellar, but now it looked so different. Bricks had been taken out of the walls, leaving dark open gaps. The floor had been dug up too.

I knew then that, once again, I had changed time. People had been digging here. Eleanor's body had been found. And most importantly, there was no presence here now. The cellar was clear of her. I looked at my arm. There was no bandage there. I had no stitches. Nor was there a plaster on my other arm.

Everything was changed.

My heart was ready to burst. I stood up, unsteady on my feet. I couldn't wait to get out of here, find out what else had changed. Afraid to believe I had done it once again. I took the steps two at a time, and threw up the hatch. Light and air streamed in. I took a deep breath and stepped up into the hall.

There were boxes piled up everywhere. The kitchen door was open, the doors to the garden lay wide. I could smell the wonderful scent of the sea. In the kitchen the cupboard doors were all open, and the shelves were bare. More boxes sat on the worktops. *Handle with Care* marked clearly on each of them. This house was being emptied. Someone was moving out. But which someone? My aunt Belle, or my gran?

Then I heard singing somewhere in the house.

'Yesterday.' The strains of it floated towards me. My gran's favourite Beatles song.

My gran. She was in this house, singing, alive. My legs felt weak now at the thought of seeing her again.

I had changed things once more, stopped my gran from falling in the cellar, stopped her from dying, because she wasn't meant to die when she did. She had more years to live with us. With me.

'Gran?' I called out, but she didn't stop singing, busy in the front room packing more boxes. I longed to see her face again. I stumbled through the hall.

I saw the shadow of her, and stopped dead. She was

holding a glass vase up to the sun and a prism of light exploded around the walls, and all the while she was singing.

I burst into the room. 'Gran!'

And she stopped singing and she turned round to me.

But it wasn't Gran.

It was Aunt Belle.

And the world began to spin. I slumped to the floor.

I came to with Aunt Belle's face close to mine, all concern. 'Honey!' She was patting my face gently. I felt a cold cloth on my brow. 'Can you sit up?'

She helped me to my shaky feet and settled me gently on a chair. 'I knew this would be too much for a young girl like you,' she said. 'Too much has happened in this awful house. I shouldn't have let you come.'

She looked around the room at the boxes and things on the floor. 'It's just we've got so little time to get all this stuff sorted before the removal men come.'

'Removal men?' I was trying desperately to catch up.

She looked at me, a puzzled frown on her face. An arched eyebrow, a lipsticked mouth, her make-up, her blonde wig. How could I ever have mistaken her for Gran? It was because I had hoped – wanted it so much.

'Well, I certainly want all our things out before they demolish the house.'

Now I was lost again. 'Demolish?'

'Raze it to the ground,' she said dramatically. 'And a good thing too. With the history this house has got it's better for it to be destroyed, obliterated, wiped off the face of the earth.' She said it with such an angry passion, she didn't sound like my funny aunt Belle. 'It would only become an attraction for ghoulish tourists. A body in the cellar! I still can't get over it.' She was talking to me as if I knew everything already. 'And your gran slept here with all that buried beneath her in that cellar.'

'Where's Gran?' My mind was still wrapped in a mist.

Aunt Belle leaned down to me and held my hand. 'We both know where she is, honey. She's in heaven now. You can be sure of that. She opened the door of heaven when she found out who that evil woman actually was – when she made sure that poor old dear at last had a decent burial.' Aunt Belle shivered, as if the thought froze her blood. 'Your gran's a heroine, Tyler. No, we know exactly where she is. Heaven, with all the other angels.' She smiled.

She thought those words would comfort me and

maybe in another time they would have. But not now –
now, all I could think was, *She's dead*. After everything
I'd done, my gran was still dead.

She had told the world about Sister Kelly, but the part
of the past I most wanted to change hadn't happened. I
hadn't brought my gran back.

Aunt Belle saw my tears. 'Come on, we're getting out
of here. We've done enough.' She pulled me to my feet.
'We'll go home and make a nice cup of tea.'

'Home?'

'Home. To your own house! And you can call your
mum and dad. They'll be in Sydney now.'

Mum and Dad in Australia – that hadn't changed.

'And Steven will be back on Friday. I think he's run
out of money.'

Steven had still gone off to Blackpool with his mates,
and Aunt Belle had still come over from New York to
spend time with me and clear the house.

Some things had changed and others had stayed the
same.

'And remember, all your friends will be home from
their vacations in a couple of days.'

My friends were coming home, and I had missed them
so much. I stood by the car watching Aunt Belle lock the

174

door of Mille Failte. The sign was still there. Such a lovely bungalow, with honeysuckle climbing round the door. A picture postcard kind of house, hiding such a wicked secret.

'At least now the evil's gone from it,' I said, as Aunt Belle started the car and we began to drive down the track to the main road.

She sighed. 'I hope so.'

35

Mum phoned us later that day. I cried when I spoke to her. I'd tried not to. I didn't want to worry her. She was so excited at seeing Sydney Opera House for the first time, calling me as she sat on the steps outside. But I just couldn't stop the tears.

'I'll be home soon, Tyler. I knew I should never have left while that blinking house was being knocked down.'

'Mum, I'm OK. Honest. Aunt Belle and I are fine.'

And by the time Aunt Belle and I had made spaghetti and meatballs for tea, I had almost come to terms with a lot of what had happened. I'd seen the press cuttings Aunt Belle had proudly kept.

HOUSE OF EVIL

The Angel of Mercy who was really the Angel of Death

And there was the grainy photo of Sister Kelly, the one Gran had left for me to find. They had discovered that Sister Kelly really was the same person as all those other nurses. Mary Duff, Catherine Macey, Margaret Campbell, Mary Cameron, Dorothy Blake and Sister Kelly – they were all one and the same evil woman. They had dug Sister Kelly up and found the DNA evidence to prove it.

We had got her in the end, my gran and I.

I figured out a lot of things that night. The spirit of Sister Kelly had lain dormant, her secret undisturbed, until Gran came with her latent psychic ability and had felt the evil in that house. Somehow, somewhere, she had found the photograph and she had begun to investigate Sister Kelly, digging out the truth, piece by piece. And that was when Sister Kelly had manifested herself in all her evil. She had come back with a vengeance to protect her vile past. She had stopped Gran from exposing her secrets. And now I knew for certain, it had been Gran who had made sure I would stay there, using everything to keep me in that house, so I would change the past and give her the time to root out the truth. Gran was as strong in death as Sister Kelly, but her strength was used for good, not evil.

My gran. There was a lovely photograph of her on the front page of one of the papers. She had gone to the authorities, told them of her suspicions that the remains of a body were in the cellar and that she knew the real identity of Sister Kelly. Things had happened very quickly after that. All Sister Kelly's secrets began to tumble like dominoes, one after another.

Poor Eleanor. She had escaped and tried to tell the world what was really happening at Mille Failte, and no one would listen. So easy to dismiss the rantings of a confused old woman. They had taken Eleanor back to her terrible fate. Eleanor, whose spirit had stayed there to make someone listen, to make someone believe her at last.

My gran smiled out at me from the front page of the paper, and that smile reassured me. She seemed to be saying, 'You and I, Tyler, we beat her. We beat Sister Kelly.'

I had achieved that at least. I had given her those extra few days she needed to expose Sister Kelly.

'It's so good to see you smiling again,' Aunt Belle said as we sat with our hot chocolate before bed.

'I'm so proud of Gran, Aunt Belle,' I said.

'Me too. She was always the strong one. My big sister.

178

She'd be so happy that you and I are sitting here and we get on so well.'

'Yes, but it would have been so much better if you and she had been able to spend all those happy times together in the house of your dreams.'

Aunt Belle scoffed at that. 'With a dead body down in the cellar. I don't think so. That house is better gone. In two days the bulldozers move in.' She sighed. 'End of a dream, Tyler.'

End of a nightmare, I was thinking.

And then I asked the question that had been bothering me all day. 'Aunt Belle, what did you mean today, when I said at least the evil's gone from that house and you said, "I hope so"? You can't think there's any evil there now?'

She took a long sip of her hot chocolate. 'I shouldn't be saying this to you, and don't tell your mum I said this. But, you know how I'm a little psychic too?' I tried not to smile. She said it so seriously, but I knew there wasn't a psychic bone in my lovely aunt Belle's body. Imagination, that's what she had. Lots of imagination.

She went on. 'I couldn't say this to your mum. Anything like that freaks your mum out – she would never listen to me.'

'Listen about what, Aunt Belle?'

'I told your gran she should move out of that house right away. As soon as she told the police of her suspicions, she should have been out of that place, not spend another second in that house. But, of course, I was only the little sister, the one with the imagination. She wouldn't listen to me. She said she didn't intend to move out until they started digging the cellar up.' Aunt Belle hesitated. 'You're the only one I could tell this to, Tyler, honey, but I think there was something evil in that house, had to be. And your gran stayed there one night too many.'

I lay in bed thinking over what Aunt Belle had said. And I knew it was true. Sister Kelly didn't get Gran in the cellar, but she got her later, that final night in Mille Failte. And I knew something else. She was still there. In that house. Waiting. Waiting for me.

I knew too I was going to go back, as soon as Aunt Belle was safely asleep.

I thought about it for a long time as I lay there, listening for Aunt Belle's gentle snoring. Yes, I was going to go back.

I would have my revenge.

36

There was no other way to get to Mille Failte at this time
of night except by taxi. I waited till I was well away from
our house before I took out my mobile and called the
taxi number.

I didn't have long to wait till a taxi picked me up. The
driver had a big smile on his face. 'You're out late for a
young lassie.'

'I know,' I said, slipping into the back seat. 'My mum's
going to kill me.'

One thing about our local taxi drivers, they loved to
chat. He turned to me and grinned. 'Och, don't worry.
She'll only shout and bawl at you and then just be relieved
you're still alive.' He began to drive, still talking, glancing
at me now and then in his rear-view mirror. 'You'll have
been at your pals', eh? Lost track of time. I was young
myself once.' He was giving me a cover story for this

imaginary mum without me saying a word. 'Just tell your mammy the truth. Because mothers have a knack of seeing through lies.' I let him talk. He was helping me forget what lay ahead of me. 'Now, where exactly are you going?'

Of course I couldn't tell him the truth. Couldn't admit I was going to that infamous house in the middle of the night. So I gave him an address on the coast road. Somewhere he could drop me. But the address was close enough to impress him. 'Wow! What do you think of that house on the shore, eh? Mille Failte? He was shaking his head. 'What was going on in that house and not a soul knew about it. Not till that old lady comes along and gets suspicious, and finds out the truth. Better than Miss Marple, eh?'

Yes, I thought, *better than Miss Marple*.

'I'll wait till you get into the house, hen,' he said when he pulled up at the address I had given him. I couldn't think of an excuse to send him away, so I opened the gate, walked up the drive and pretended to ring the bell. I turned and waved at him, but still he stayed, his pleasant face still smiling. I wished he would go, though I knew he was only anxious for my safety. Then he pointed upstairs and I looked up and my heart sank. A light had come on in an upstairs room. Panic must have shown on

182

my face, because he gave me the thumbs-up and winked. 'Remember. Tell the truth.'

I sighed with relief when I heard another call coming in to him on his radio. He threw me another wave, and then he was gone.

I have never moved so fast. I was down that path and out of the gate seconds after he sped away. I saw his tail lights disappearing round the bend in the road. Only then did I cross the street and head for the house.

It lay still and silent, and though I held my breath and listened hard there was no sound, no feeling of a malevolent presence. Yet, I knew she was here, waiting for me. Her next victim. Her final victim. And I knew where I would find her.

I opened the door and walked into the hall. My step was steady and firm as I made my way to that room, the room where she died.

The green chair still sat in that corner and the bed was bare now, with only a mattress, but otherwise there was no other furniture here, just some boxes piled up by the door. Tomorrow, the removal men would come and clear the house of everything before it was obliterated from the face of the earth.

What I had to do must be done tonight.

*　*　*

I lay on the bed on my back and stared at the ceiling. The door of the room swung slowly shut.

The room grew darker. The only sound was the beating of my heart.

Gran, I prayed to her. *Gran, give me strength. For tonight. Give me all your strength.*

And the shadow in the chair began to stir.

37

I saw it move, a shadow without shape – stirring into some kind of life from that spot where she had died. I turned my head for a moment, dared to look at the way that shadow seemed to sway and flow and, though I could make out no face, I knew a face was there.

And now it was coming for me.

I snapped my eyes away, turned them to the ceiling, and lay there, my arms crossed in front of me, like a corpse myself, rigid with terror. But there was something else stronger in me than fear. Determination. I closed my eyes tight shut. Sewed them closed with invisible thread, so they would stay shut no matter what. I felt that dark shape close in. I imagined it swirling like smoke towards the bed, willing me to look. And I knew if I did, it would be watching me, triumphant.

It was beside the bed now. If I dared reach out my hand, I would be able to touch it. Sink my hand into its evil. But still I didn't move.

It shifted again. I felt the cold of it rising above me, hovering over me. I could feel the black coldness of it weigh heavy on me, envelop me. And still I did not look.

Closer it came, lowering itself on top of me, until I could feel its dead, icy breath against my face, smell the rotting evil of it in my nostrils. I held my breath and it came closer. So close now, urging me to open my eyes and see. Daring me to look.

My heart was racing, and now there was no way I could stop myself. My eyes slowly opened.

And I was looking into the face of evil.

The eyes burning, the mouth wide. And that face broke into the mockery of a smile. A smile of triumph because she had forced me to look into her face.

She roared and I heard again that sound. A sound that seemed to rise from the depths. Her shadow covered me. She thought she'd won.

Think again, Sister Kelly.

I stared back into those eyes. I did not flinch. I opened my mouth as wide as hers. And with every bit of strength

I had, I roared back at her. My eyes as wild as hers – wild because she had killed my grandmother.

At my roar she shrank back, and I knelt up on the bed and roared again and she moved away and now I followed her, and my roar became a yell, a yell of triumph.

'Do your worst, Sister Kelly. I live. You died.' And I roared again, and the black shadow moved back against the door.

She was building her strength. Getting ready to come at me again, and I was so afraid I had no strength left to fight her. I watched the power in her grow. But I knelt on the bed, my back straight, waiting for her. Afraid as I was, I would not let my gran down.

At that moment the whole house seemed to shake. The floor trembled. My eyes never left her and it seemed she had felt that movement too for those eyes left me. I followed her gaze then, and it was as if the floor was coming alive. Something was rising through the floor-boards, something black and menacing. And now I saw that it wasn't me who was afraid.

It was her.

Those eyes were wild with terror. The blackness rising from the floor became shapes, malevolent shapes, and they surrounded her. She had nowhere to go. Something more evil, something stronger than her was here. She tried to struggle. I could see how she struggled but they held her fast. She could not escape. And I knew in that instant what they were and why they had come for her.

'Take her!' I screamed it. 'Take her. I win, Sister Kelly. Can you hear me? I. Win.'

And her roar became a whimper as they pulled her down. Inch by inch she oozed down through the floor, and I had no pity for her who had been pitiless to so many.

With one final cry of terror she was gone. And the cold of the room went with her.

I sat back on my heels and looked around me.

She was gone.

The house was free of her.

And so was I.

38

Crowds came to see the demolition. It was a media event and a real tourist attraction. Television cameras were there, and reporters from all the national newspapers. My friends and I watched it all safely behind the yellow police tape there to hold the crowds back.

I watched Aunt Belle. She had already been interviewed by several television reporters. She was in her element, glowing with pride for her sister. She had bought a new wig especially for the event.

'I'm glad I'm back for this,' Jazz said. 'I wouldn't have missed it for the world.'

Aisha giggled. 'Nor me. How often are we in the middle of a murder mystery?'

More often than you think, Aisha, I could have told her, but she would never know. None of them would. This gift I had would also be my secret.

'I feel bad we've been off on holiday and you've been stuck here,' Jazz said. 'You must have been so bored, just packing up an old house.'

'Yes,' I said, holding back a smile. 'Really bored.'

It was then I saw Paul Forbes pushing his way through the crowd. I stared at him. Couldn't help it.

'Do you know him?' Mac said, his gaze following mine. There was a hint of jealousy in his tone, and I liked that.

'Who is he? He's kind of dishy?' Jazz said. Paul was. I could appreciate his good looks now – his soft brown hair and those brown eyes. It was hard to forget that the last time I had seen him he'd had a look of stark terror on his face.

'Dishy, but a bit rude.' Aisha tapped him on the shoulder. 'Excuse me, you're blocking our view.'

Paul turned, and he looked straight at me for just a second. I smiled, because he had been kind enough to stay with my aunt. He had helped me. He smiled back at me, but there was no recognition on his face at all. 'Sorry,' he said, and he moved aside.

'Are you sure you don't know him?' Mac asked again.

'Don't get your boxers in a twist. You're still her boyfriend. That right, Tyler?' Jazz said.

I laughed, and Mac smiled at me.

'Though I am getting her checked out to see if there is any insanity in her family,' Jazz said. And we all laughed.

Aisha squeezed my arm. 'Are you all right about watching this?'

'Me? I'm fine.'

Better than fine, I was thinking. I had learned a lot about myself these past few weeks. I could change the past. And I would again. There were others out there. The people I saw in my dreams. The unlawfully dead. Asking for my help. And I would help them, though I would be afraid, even terrified. If I had a gift, this was it.

I could not turn away.

I would not turn away.

And at that moment the bulldozers moved in.

And the house fell down.

Loved SECRET OF THE SHADOWS?

Then read on to find out about Cathy MacPhail and her gripping stories

Meet Cathy MacPhail

Cathy MacPhail was born and brought up in Greenock, Scotland, where she still lives. Before becoming a children's author, she wrote short stories for magazines and comedy programmes for radio. Cathy was inspired to write her first children's book after her daughter was bullied at school.

Cathy writes spooky thrillers for younger readers as well as teen novels. She has won the Royal Mail Book Award twice, along with lots of other awards. She loves to give her readers a 'rattling good read' and has been called the Scottish Jacqueline Wilson.

One of Cathy's greatest fears would be to meet another version of herself, similar to the young girl in her bestselling novel *Another Me*. She is a big fan of *Doctor Who* and would love to write a scary monster episode for the series.

Cathy loves to hear from her fans, so visit **www.cathymacphail.com** and email her your thoughts.

Questions from Cathy's fans!

I love reading your books but what do you love reading?

There are so many fantastic books out there that I read all kinds of things. Have you read anything by Robert Swindells? I love his work. He writes the kind of books I like to read. *Room 13* is genuinely spooky!

Where do you get the ideas for your characters?

I get my ideas from real life – watching, listening, observing. I met a teacher who said that if he could take a group of boys out on the mountains for a few days, they would come back different people. He became Mr Marks in *Underworld*; I saw an item in a newspaper about a gangland boss who ruled with fear and he became Armour in *Grass*; I was at a school event, signing books, and a girl walked to the front of the queue. Everyone complained, and all she said was, 'The line starts behind me.' And it did. Fiona from *Underworld* was born. A spark of someone can inspire a great character.

And, of course, I met a girl at a school in Falkirk, called Tyler Lawless! There's no need to tell you which character she inspired.

If you could be a character in one of your books, who would you be, and why?

Ooh! Two answers here, I think. I loved Ram in the *Nemesis* series. I think he was brave and adventurous and good-hearted. I'd like to be any of those. Also, Fiona out of *Underworld* is my alter ego. I love how she always says the right thing at the right time. I never do that. It's always *after* someone's insulted me that I think up a good retort.

Do you plan each story before you begin writing or does the story take shape as you write?

Most of the time, the story takes shape in my head! When I get the idea, I can't stop thinking about it. That's what happened with *Secret of the Shadows*. I passed an isolated little bungalow on the coastal road near where I live, and straight away I imagined it was haunted by something evil. But what? I knew I wanted Tyler Lawless to help solve that mystery, so over the next few days I kept writing down all the spooky things that could happen to her in that house. Once I had a lot of the content, I wrote the outline for the story and developed it into a more detailed synopsis of the plot. The way I work out all my books is to then divide the synopsis into exciting, creepy chapters. I think of it like going on a trip. I usually know where I am going to end up, but I might take some thrilling detours along the way.

If you weren't a writer, what would you be?
I love anything weird and mysterious. So, if I was brave enough, I would love to have been an adventurer who explores myths and legends, stories about ghosts and strange creatures, and unsolved mysteries. But I probably wouldn't be brave enough!

These questions have been provided by Cathy's readers. If you would like to ask Cathy a question to feature in her forthcoming books, or you just want to let Cathy know what you think of her stories, please email your questions and thoughts to **childrensmarketing@ bloomsbury.com**.

OUT OF THE DEPTHS

Read on for a spine-tingling taster
of another story featuring Tyler Lawless,
a brave and feisty sleuth with a very special gift

I saw my teacher in the queue at the supermarket last Christmas. Miss Baxter. I was surprised to see her. She'd been dead for six months.

She saw me. I know she saw me. In fact, I could swear her eyes were searching me out. As if she was watching for me.

As if she'd been waiting for me.

I hurried towards her, pushing people aside, but you know what it's like at Christmas. Queues at all the checkouts, crowds with trolleys piled high with shopping, everything and everyone blocking your way. By the time I got to where I'd seen her, she was gone. No sign of her anywhere.

And when I told them at school no one would believe me. 'Typical Tyler Lawless,' they all said. 'You're always making up stories.'

Even my best friend, Annabelle, agreed with them. She'd sounded annoyed at me. Wanted me to be just an ordinary, run-of-the-mill best friend who didn't cause her any embarrassment.

I had let my imagination run away with me, everyone said. It was just another of my stories. It's true I want to be a writer, and I do look for stories everywhere. You're supposed to do that. But this time I wasn't making it up. I really did see her.

Miss Baxter had died abroad during the summer holidays. A tragic accident, they said. An accident that should never have happened. Her body had been brought back and she was buried somewhere in England.

But I had seen her!

I couldn't stop thinking about her. Trying to find an explanation for the unexplainable. And I began to think . . . what if she hadn't died at all? What if someone else's body had been identified as hers? What if it was all a scam to get the life insurance?

Or what if she was in the witness protection programme and had had to change her identity?

'She'd hardly be likely to pop into the local supermarket then, would she?' Annabelle scoffed at me. And if she couldn't believe me, what chance did I have with anyone else?

I had also seen Miss Baxter making furtive calls. At least to me they looked furtive. Snapping her phone shut when she had seen I was watching her. And I thought, what if she had a secret life, was an undercover agent, and she'd come to the school for some dark purpose? And then had to fake her own death so she could move on to her next assignment.

It was those 'what-ifs' that were always getting me

into trouble. My imagination had caused me a mountain of problems at my last school.

I saw the French assistant, Mademoiselle Carlier, and the new science teacher going home together in her car one night after school. I had noticed them before, sharing a look, a smile when they thought no one was watching. But the science teacher was married.

'What if they're having an affair?' I whispered.

I whispered it to the wrong person. She passed it on and I was pulled into the head's office and warned about spreading rumours. That had been my first warning. The first of many.

But it was this story, this one in particular, my insistence that I had seen Miss Baxter, that had caused the most trouble. I wouldn't let it go. I wouldn't let them say I was making it up. I *had* seen her. It hadn't been a mistake. I began to get angry when people ridiculed me. And that just got me into more trouble.

My parents finally decided it would be best to take me out of that school and find somewhere else. It was a case of leaving before I was pushed. I was already on my final warning by this time. Unfair, in my opinion. I never caused real trouble. I wasn't a bully. I was never disruptive

. . . I just noticed things other people missed. And, in the end, I had been right about Mademoiselle Carlier. Her and the science teacher had run off together, causing no end of scandal. But, of course, no one remembered that! Oh no. In fact, it only seemed to make things worse. As if by telling people about my suspicions I had actually made it happen. As if *I'd* done something wrong.

Sleekit, one of the teachers called me.

Sleekit. A great Scottish word – it means sly and underhand and untrustworthy. A great word, but not when it was applied to me. It hurt. I wasn't sleekit at all.

I had promised myself that here, in this new school, St Anthony's College, things were going to be different . . .

Prepared to be thrilled with more seriously spooky stories from Cathy MacPhail

OUT NOW